"I'm taking you back to my house and locking you in."

"Lock me in? Not a chance. In fact, I think I'll run back over to the crime scene."

"The hell you will. Okay fine. We'll review the files together."

"Good. I'm glad you finally see it my way."

Cade shook his head. "Trust me, Gillespie. I do *not* see it your way. That's not why I'm doing this."

"It's not? Then why are you?"

"Maybe it doesn't mean much to you that someone's obviously trying to harm you, but it does to me."

That stopped her. Laurel's eyes widened. "It does?"

"Yeah." Feeling flayed open by his unintentional revelation, he scrambled to think of a flip answer. "Yeah. Because if anyone around here is going to shoot or strangle you, it's going to be me."

MALLORY KANE

HIGH SCHOOL REUNION

TORONTO • NEW YORK • LONDON
AMSTERDAM • PARIS • SYDNEY • HAMBURG
STOCKHOLM • ATHENS • TOKYO • MILAN • MADRID
PRAGUE • WARSAW • BUDAPEST • AUCKLAND

For my brave, heroic mother.
Mama, I miss you every day.

Recycling programs
for this product may
not exist in your area.

ISBN-13: 978-0-373-69370-2
ISBN-10: 0-373-69370-2

HIGH SCHOOL REUNION

www.eHarlequin.com

Printed in U.S.A.

ABOUT THE AUTHOR

Mallory Kane credits her love of books to her mother, a librarian, who taught her that books are a precious resource and should be treated with loving respect. Her grandfather and her father were steeped in the Southern tradition of oral history, and they could hold an audience spellbound with their storytelling skills. Mallory aspires to be as good a storyteller as her father. She loves romantic suspense with dangerous heroes and dauntless heroines, and often uses her medical background to add an extra dose of intrigue to her books. Mallory lives in Mississippi with her computer-genius husband, their two fascinating cats, and, at current count, seven computers.

She loves to hear from readers. You can write her at mallory@mallorykane.com or care of Harlequin Books.

Books by Mallory Kane

*Ultimate Agents

CAST OF CHARACTERS

Cade Dupree—When his older brother died and his dad had a stroke, Dusty Springs Police Chief Cade Dupree gave up his FBI career to return home for his father's sake.

Laurel Gillespie—A forensic criminologist with the FBI's Division of Unsolved Mysteries in Washington, D.C.

Kathy Adler—A closet alcoholic and the leader of the Cool Girls clique in high school, Kathy has the other girls under her thumb. Did she use them to pull off the ultimate humiliation of a geeky classmate—a faked suicide that was really murder?

Mary Sue Nelson—One of the Cool Girls. Is her silly, blond-bimbo persona real, or a clever act that hides a sinister intelligence?

Debra Honeycutt—Quiet and sweet, Cool Girl Debra may have been caught up in a high-school prank gone bad. But someone thinks she knows too much.

Sheryl Posey—The fourth Cool Girl is a cagey survivor who figured out a long time ago that survival meant becoming a hired gun. Whoever can do her the most good gets her loyalty. Did she kill to protect what she knows?

Ralph Langston—A self-remade high school nerd wanted the prestigious Science Medal for himself. Was he jealous enough to commit murder and cover it up as a suicide? Or is he just an opportunist cashing in on another's secret?

Ann Noble—The super-efficient secretary to the mayor of Dusty Springs hides a lot under her practical suits and glasses. But does she know anything about the death or is she bluffing?

Chapter One

FBI Special Agent Laurel Gillespie rang her friend's doorbell for the third time.

"Come on, Misty," she muttered. "Answer the door."

She rested her hand on her Glock .23 and eyed the carved, wooden front door. No way could she break it down. But she remembered from childhood that the Wallers' back door was half glass—one quick whack with the butt of her gun and she could be inside.

She rubbed the back of her neck. It had been prickling ever since she'd driven into Dusty Springs. She didn't want to be here. Didn't want to run into anyone she knew from high school.

"Come on, Misty. Where are you?" Laurel knew Misty Waller as well as she knew herself. Her best friend from grade school was dependable to a fault—practically obsessive-compulsive. It wasn't in her nature not to be where she said she'd be.

Laurel had called her as soon as she'd landed in Memphis, just like they'd agreed. But Misty hadn't answered—not her home phone or her cell.

So Laurel had picked up her rental car and driven the forty-five miles south to Dusty Springs, Mississippi, in record time. She'd called several more times, but Misty had never answered.

Something was wrong. And that was why she'd tucked her paddle holster into her waistband at the small of her back before she'd approached the door.

She rang the doorbell one last time. The chime echoed hollowly throughout the house.

She drew her weapon and carefully turned the doorknob, expecting resistance. It turned!

Instinctively, she flattened her back against the door facing as her boss's voice echoed in her ears. *Every suspicious circumstance is a crime scene until you prove it's not.*

And right now, too many things weren't adding up. Misty *never* left a door unlocked.

Carefully, she nudged the door open, cringing when the hinges creaked. She angled inside, leading with her weapon, her senses on full alert. The sight that greeted her in the foyer sent alarm thrumming through her.

Scraps of paper littered the floor, lit by the blue glow that flickered from the living room to her left.

TV with no sound. Another habit of Misty's from high school. She'd always studied in front of the TV with the sound turned off.

But not with the lights off.

Laurel pressed her back against the wall, prepared to lead with her gun. A muffled thud sent her heart rate soaring.

"FBI," she called. "I'm coming in. Identify yourself."

A plaintive yowl echoed through the doorway. A cat. *Of course.* Misty had always had a cat.

Taking a deep breath to steady her pulse, Laurel stepped around the door facing, her Glock at the ready. The cat bumped her leg.

On the floor in front of the couch, silhouetted in the

TV's eerie glow, she saw a crumpled form. Her fingers tightened on her weapon and her heart rate doubled. "Misty? Is that you?"

No response.

She fought to keep her breathing even. Training had taught her that danger sent the pulse sky high—three-hundred beats per minute or more. But training also taught her how to control it. She had to keep her cool.

She felt for the light switch but couldn't find it. Swinging her weapon around one more time, she squinted in the dim blue light. The living room looked like the day after a ticker-tape parade. Photos and scraps of paper were scattered everywhere. No sound reached her ears except the discordant hum of an ancient window air conditioner.

She eyed the body on the floor with growing apprehension. "Misty?"

Nothing. She crossed the room, careful to keep her back to the wall and her finger on the trigger. One glance at the woman's pale face and hair told her it *was* her friend. Blood blackened the left side of her head.

She held her breath and watched Misty's chest. There—a faint flutter.

Thank heavens. Misty was alive. Laurel hated to leave her friend lying in her own blood, but neglecting the basics could get them both killed.

So, gripping her weapon more tightly, Laurel edged her way through the dining room and into the kitchen. She quickly and efficiently cleared the house.

Whoever had attacked Misty was gone.

Back in the den, she knelt beside her friend. "Misty? Honey? Can you hear me?"

She didn't answer. Laurel reached for her cell phone to call 9-1-1.

"Damn it." She'd left it in the car, plugged into the charger. She glanced around. An old-fashioned dial phone sat on a side table, but from her position Laurel could see the naked wires. Whoever had attacked Misty had jerked the phone out of the wall.

She moved to stand, and the toe of her pump touched something. It was a baseball bat that had rolled partway under the couch. Laurel nudged it with her foot. There was wet, shiny blood on the end of it.

She hated to leave Misty alone, but she had to get to her phone. She had to report an assault with a deadly weapon.

Someone had attacked her friend and left her for dead.

POLICE CHIEF CADE DUPREE turned onto Misty Waller's street and parked near the corner. He'd been investigating a report of a break-in at the Visitor Center of Dusty Springs' brand new convention complex when the call came in.

Mrs. Gardner, Misty's neighbor, was frantic, because someone was lurking around their street. That was the word she'd used. *Lurking.* To hear her tell it, people had been *lurking* all afternoon.

A break-in and a *lurking* in one evening—that was more crime than he'd seen since he'd left the FBI to take over his dad's job as chief of police of Dusty Springs. His mouth curved into a wry smile as he walked down the sidewalk toward the Wallers' house.

Not quite what he'd pictured himself doing after completing his training at Quantico. Still, at least this job wasn't dangerous.

Or interesting.

A curtain fluttered in Mrs. Gardner's window. Cade resisted the urge to wave at her as he spotted a rental car parked in front of Misty's house.

That was what he'd figured. The *lurker* was a friend of Misty's in town for the high-school reunion.

He pushed up the brim of his cap and squinted in the bright sunlight. The driver's side door was open, and a well-rounded backside above long shapely legs faced him. *Not Misty.* This bottom was skinnier, sexier. And those legs…

"Evening, ma'am," he said, as he approached the front of the car.

The woman tensed, then straightened. The car's interior light glinted off blue steel.

Gun. Cade rocked to the balls of his feet and moved his hand to his belt holster. "Hold it right there."

She froze.

"Now set that gun down on the car seat and straighten up slowly."

She obeyed. As she straightened, the car's light caught coppery highlights in her collar-length hair. She held out her hands in a nonthreatening gesture.

Her brows lowered and her mouth dropped open for a split-second, but before he could wonder what she found surprising, she composed her face and looked him straight in the eye.

"It's all right," she said. "I'm FBI." She slowly pulled her jacket aside to reveal the distinctive badge pinned to her waistband.

"FBI?" Unwelcome memories assaulted his brain. The excitement of making it to Quantico. The sense of purpose that the FBI had chosen him. But then his older brother had died, his father had suffered a stroke and he'd had to give up his dream and return to Dusty Springs.

Cade forced his attention back to the woman. "What's going on?"

"Misty's hurt. I need to call 9-1-1. I left my cell phone in the car."

"I'm 9-1-1. Do we need the EMTs?"

"Yes. She's got a blow to the head."

Cade didn't stop to ask any more questions. He sprinted up the steps and through the front door.

"The living room," the woman called out.

He rounded the doorway and saw Misty crumpled on the floor. He crouched beside her. There was blood matted in her hair.

"Misty, you all right?" Damn, that was a lot of blood.

Misty stirred and moaned. Relief loosened his tight neck and shoulders. "Lie still. I'm calling an ambulance."

He punched a preset number. "Get the EMTs over here," he barked. "The Wallers' house. Misty's hurt. And no sirens. Don't wake all the neighbors."

The FBI agent's heels clicked on the hardwood floor, but Cade kept his attention on Misty. "You're doing fine, Misty. Hang in there another couple of minutes." He patted her hand, then spoke to the agent. "I don't think the injury is serious. She may have a concussion."

"The weapon's right under your feet."

"So you found her like this?"

"That's right."

"You didn't see anyone leaving the area? Didn't pass a vehicle?"

"No."

"How'd you get in?"

"The door was unlocked."

Cade swiveled and eyed her. He hadn't taken the time to examine the door. "Unlocked?"

She nodded, looking past him at Misty. "Yes. Definitely. And no sign of forced entry. It doesn't make sense. She has an obsession about locking her doors."

He heard a truck pull up outside. Within seconds,

heavy footsteps on the wooden porch announced the arrival of the EMTs.

"Here we go, Misty. They're going to take good care of you." He rose from his haunches and moved out of the way so the EMTs could check her out.

He met the FBI agent's gaze and found her watching him with a pensive expression.

She blinked, and then held out her hand. "I'm Laurel Gillespie. You don't remember me. I was a year behind you in school."

"Gillespie?" he repeated absently.

Laurel saw the blank look in Cade's eye and her heart sank. She knew he wouldn't remember her, but that didn't make it any easier.

He stepped aside as the EMTs lifted Misty onto a gurney. He was close—too close. She could smell his after-shave. It was fresh and subtle. Sexy.

Dear heavens, she was really standing next to Cade Dupree, her high-school crush. She'd thought that by now, ten years after she'd graduated from high school, she'd have forgotten his confident stance, his broad-shouldered, slim-hipped silhouette.

Now that the threat of danger and her worry about Misty were over, she was practically shaking with reaction. Partly from finding Misty collapsed and bleeding, but partly from seeing Cade.

She turned her head. His handsome, familiar face was only a few inches from hers, his thick lashes lowered as he watched Misty. He hadn't changed except that his face had more character and his body had filled out with lean, hard muscles.

Her pulse fluttered as his gaze met hers and roamed over her face. How could she still remember that voice, those long powerful legs, that lanky frame? And his sky-blue eyes. She'd swooned over those eyes in high school.

He sent her a taste of his killer smile. "So—Laurel Gillespie," he drawled, "FBI agent."

Despite the unwelcome return of her adolescent jitters, Laurel bristled at his patronizing tone. She'd thought she was prepared for Cade Dupree. She wasn't.

He straightened, and rested his hand on the butt of his gun. He was chief of police—the job his dad had held for as long as she could remember. And he was taking charge of the crime scene.

Laurel took a deep breath. She wasn't about to wait for him to order her out of the house.

"I'll take charge of the front. Keep people out." She turned on her heel without waiting for an answer.

Great. She'd put herself exactly where she didn't want to be. In full view of the entire town of Dusty Springs.

She felt like a threshold guardian as a parade of curious neighbors tried to get inside. She had no trouble flashing her badge to turn away the owner of the hardware store and his wife, or a young mother with a toddler in her arms, or a couple of teenage boys, all of whom gasped in awe when she informed them that the house was a crime scene. But she dreaded running into any of her former classmates.

Her memories of high school were of not fitting in, of the nightmare of braces and glasses, unruly red hair and painful shyness.

Within a few minutes, a familiar man in his early fifties, wearing a badge and a gun, walked up to her. Behind him, a younger man in a misbuttoned police uniform shirt carried a roll of yellow crime-scene tape.

"Evening, Laurel. That is, Special Agent Gillespie. I didn't know you were an FBI agent."

"Officer Evans, hi."

"Cade—Chief Dupree—called us to tape off the scene. He said you might need some help." He punched a thumb backward through the air. "This is Officer Shelton Phillips."

She nodded at Phillips and smiled at Officer Evans. "Thanks," she said gratefully.

Just like Cade's dad, Fred Evans had been a police officer since she could remember. His daughter Debra had belonged to the snootiest clique in school.

Officer Phillips quickly cordoned off the front of the house and then headed around back.

Laurel turned toward the dwindling crowd just as a tall woman with skinny legs and a haughty air walked up. Kathy Hodges.

Speaking of snooty. Kathy and Debra and a couple of other girls had named themselves the Cool Girls. The rest of the class called them the *CeeGees.* They'd made it their mission to target certain classmates, usually the shyest ones, to humiliate and embarrass.

Laurel's confidence drained away as scenes from the most embarrassing night of her life swept through her head with the clarity of a high-definition movie.

Afterward, she'd kicked herself for not seeing through the cruel prank. But on the night of the Homecoming Dance her sophomore year, she'd really believed that senior football captain James Dupree, who was the Homecoming King, wanted *her* to dance the traditional first dance with him. Although she was smitten with James's younger brother Cade, there was no way she would pass up the biggest honor in a sophomore girl's year.

Remembered excitement and apprehension swirled through her as she relived that awful moment. Standing on the dance floor in a brand new gown, clutching the note from James in her hand.

Please do me the honor of dancing the first dance with me.

Her heart fluttering as James's cocky gaze swept the room, stopping to wink at her.

Then he held out his hand and smiled. And Laurel had started climbing the stairs to the stage.

Still smiling at her, James named another girl. Everyone's laughter still rang in her ears. By the next morning, it was all over school and Laurel was humiliated.

Now here she was, facing Kathy for the first time since she'd graduated and moved away with her parents. Despite her success, she suddenly felt like the plain, shy girl she'd been ten years ago.

Kathy's blond hair was sleek and newly colored, her makeup was perfect, but her eyes were bloodshot, and not even expensive makeup could hide all the tiny veins visible around her nose. A lit cigarette smoldered in her perfectly manicured hand. She looked thin and pinched and miserable.

Laurel stood straighter as Kathy walked purposefully up the steps.

"Pardon me," Kathy said, waving the hand that held the cigarette. Even with the cigarette smoke, Laurel could smell whiskey on her breath.

"Sorry, Kathy. This is a crime scene. No one's allowed inside."

Kathy's perfectly shaped brows drew down as she eyed Laurel. "Nonsense. Misty's my friend."

Doubt it, Laurel thought.

Kathy made a shooing gesture toward Laurel. "Check with Cade—Police Chief Dupree. Now excuse me."

Laurel's initial flutter of apprehension at facing Kathy

evaporated in a flash of anger. She held her badge in front of Kathy's face.

"Sorry, Kathy. FBI. Please step back."

"Who the hell *are* you?" Kathy nervously flicked ash off her cigarette.

"Special Agent Laurel Gillespie." She met Kathy's hard green gaze and was rewarded by a look of frank shock.

Just as Fred Evans walked up, Kathy recovered.

"You have *got* to be kidding." She tried to sidestep Laurel.

"Hold it, Kathy," Officer Evans said, taking her arm.

Kathy looked down at his hand. "You don't want to do that, Fred."

Laurel frowned. Were Kathy's words slurred? She'd smelled the booze on her breath. But was she really drunk at just after eight in the evening?

"One word to Harrison and you—" Kathy pointed her cigarette at Fred, "will be facing assault charges." That came out as *ashault sharges*.

"Right." His brown eyes twinkled as he glanced at Laurel. "Your husband's a real estate attorney. Come on, let's take you home. All the excitement's over. I'll tell Harrison to get you into bed." He gestured to Officer Phillips.

"Oh, please, Fred. Harrison hasn't gotten me into bed in two years."

"Shelton, walk Mrs. Adler home and make sure Harrison's there. I'll stay here in case the chief needs anything else."

Phillips led Kathy away.

Laurel didn't have any more trouble, although several more people she'd known in high school showed up. Obviously, word still spread as fast as it always had in Dusty Springs.

Within a couple of minutes, the EMTs rolled Misty out

on a gurney. Fred and Phillips and a couple of guys they'd recruited kept the rubberneckers at bay as the EMTs loaded Misty into the ambulance.

Static erupted from Fred's radio. He listened, said something, and then walked up the steps.

"I've got everything under control out here, Agent Gillespie," Fred said. "Chief Dupree wants you inside."

"Thanks. But please call me Laurel. It's good to see you. So you're working with Cade now."

He chuckled and nodded. "Yep. Worked for his dad and now for him. Kind of a tradition in Dusty Springs I guess."

"How is Debra?"

His chuckle faded. "She's fine. Cade's waiting for you."

Laurel thanked him again and went inside. The living room's overhead light was on. It spotlighted the scrapbooks and photo albums that were torn and tossed all over the floor amidst dozens of loose photos and piles of books.

Somebody had been looking for something, and Laurel was afraid she knew what it was. The question was, had they found it?

Cade's head turned a few degrees. "I guess you're here for the reunion. You were in Misty's class, right? How'd you happen to turn up just in time?"

He faced the back of the couch, looking down at the spot where Misty had lain. Laurel had her first fully lighted view of him.

Her mouth went dry and her throat fluttered, just like in high school. Most of the girls in Dusty Springs would have given their eyeteeth for a smile from his brother James, but it was Cade who'd always been able to stop her heart.

He filled up the room, just like he always had. He'd never been as big or tall as James. And while James's sparkling personality and talent in sports made him the envy of every guy and the heartthrob of every girl in town, Laurel had always preferred Cade's quiet good looks and shy smile.

She blinked, and the image of the boy turned into the reality of the man.

He stood, legs hip-width apart. Worn, perfectly fitting jeans emphasized his buttocks and muscled thighs. His fists were propped on his hips, which pulled the cotton of his Ole Miss T-shirt tight across his back. Under his baseball cap, his brown hair was dark with sweat.

He was surveying the crime scene, which was what she should be doing.

She forced her gaze away from him and looked at the floor where Misty had lain. Her brain queued up a stop-action movie of the crime, based on Misty's position, the blood spatter and the condition of the house.

She put herself into the head of the attacker. *I sneak up behind Misty and hit her while she's sitting on the couch.*

No. If Misty had been sitting, she'd have slumped over *onto* the couch, not fallen on the floor in front of it.

Cade turned his head and pinned her with his electric-blue gaze. "My question wasn't rhetorical."

She forced herself not to look away. "I didn't think it was. What do you think about her position on the floor?"

"I asked you first."

"Fair enough." She stepped closer. "Yes, I'm here for the reunion. I flew in to Memphis this afternoon and drove straight here."

"Flew in from where?"

"D.C. I work at FBI Headquarters. I'm a criminologist with the Division of Unsolved Mysteries."

His gaze sharpened, but all he did was nod.

"Misty invited me to stay with her. I tried to call her several times, on her cell and her home phone, but she never answered, which was odd since she'd made me promise to call. I pulled into her driveway at 8:03 p.m. Rang her bell, knocked on the door, then drew my weapon and turned the knob. It was unlocked."

Cade turned around and crossed his arms. "You said that. Do you know how unlikely that is? Misty's—"

"Borderline agoraphobic. I know." She nodded. "Not to mention a tad obsessive-compulsive. Even in grade school she couldn't stand to be inside a house alone with the doors unlocked."

"Which means either she let someone in or they picked the lock."

"That lock's at least sixty years old. It could probably be opened with a credit card."

"So you walked into a dark house that you knew shouldn't be unlocked, not knowing whether you'd find a burglar, a murderer or a rapist?"

"Or my best friend from high school." Laurel kept her expression neutral, but it was an effort. "I'm a trained agent with field and crime-scene experience. I know how to enter a suspicious dwelling."

His face darkened. "Without backup?"

Laurel shrugged. She knew he was right to question her, but she wasn't wrong. Not totally. She let it drop. "So what do you think about her position?"

"Someone conked her from behind."

"While she was sitting on the couch?"

"Nope. She'd have slumped over."

Images of what must have happened played out in Laurel's head. "Picture this." She turned to look at the foyer door. "I come in the door. Either it's unlocked—doubtful—or I somehow unlock it without Misty hearing me." She stepped toward the couch and raised her hand.

"I'm holding the baseball bat. Did I bring it in or pick it up here?"

Cade still had his arms crossed. He nodded toward the couch. "I'm thinking the bat was Misty's. It was probably near the front door—for protection."

"What did you do with it?"

"I gave it to Shelton—Officer Phillips—to check for prints."

"Okay, I'm holding the bat. I raise my arm and swing—" She demonstrated.

"What are you doing?"

The scene in her head freeze-framed. She looked up at him. "Trying to get a picture of what happened."

"You do realize you're talking as if you're the attacker?"

"Oh. A lot of the time I work alone, looking at forensic evidence from photographs or video. I talk to myself."

His brows drew down. "So you walk in the perp's shoes. I reckon I see the crime unfolding like a movie—it's how my dad always did it. I guess everybody's got their own way of doing things." He scrutinized her. "So, Gillespie, if you're acting out what the attacker did, you need to use your other hand. The blow was to the left side of Misty's head."

She felt her cheeks heat up. "You're right. The attacker had to be left-handed." She looked at her hands. "Wouldn't you think at least one perp would use the wrong hand, just to throw off the police?"

Cade's mouth turned up at the corner and Laurel's pulse jumped at the hint of his killer smile.

He shrugged. "Plus you've still got Misty sitting on the couch."

"Okay. Let's start over." She started to turn back toward the door.

"Hold it." Cade stopped her with a hand on her arm. A large, blunt-fingered, warm hand.

Crime scene, she thought. Crime scene, not high school.

"Are you planning to act out the entire thing?"

"I like to when I can."

He cocked his head to one side. "Okay, go ahead."

She gave him a sheepish smile. "Why did Misty get up? Did she hear something and turn around? Here. You be the attacker and I'll be Misty."

Cade sent her a look. "Might as well. We don't have much else to go on. Shelton lifted prints off the dining table, but Misty had a reunion committee meeting here a couple of days ago, so there are going to be dozens of prints."

"It was three days ago. You stand here, behind the couch." She moved to go around to the front but Cade caught her arm again.

"Aren't you going to give me the blunt object?"

"Ha ha. Don't make fun of me unless you have a better idea."

He shook his head.

"Here's something else to think about. Look at the couch."

"Yeah, I know. Blood spatter across the cushions. Proves she wasn't sitting."

"Have you taken samples?"

"Got a few. Don't forget that this isn't D.C. It's Dusty Springs, Mississippi. We're not equipped to handle a lot of lab work, and I can guarantee you that the state lab won't consider a minor breaking and entering, even with injuries, top priority."

Laurel didn't comment. She knew she could use the FBI lab in D.C., but if she offered, Cade would want to know why she'd use their resources for such a relatively insignificant crime. And she wasn't ready to explain the reason she'd violated her promise to herself never to set foot in Dusty Springs again. She knew the suspicion that had drawn her back here was flimsy at best. She needed to gain Cade's confidence before she told him her theory.

"Okay," she said. "I'm sitting on the couch, watching TV. I hear something. I get up and turn around. It would explain the blow to the left side of her head—"

Cade swung the imaginary bat. "But not her position on the floor."

"Use your left hand." Air stirred against her cheek as he feigned a blow to the left side of her head. "I crumple into the exact position where she was found."

"So she had to be facing the TV."

"But if she stood because she heard the intruder, why *didn't* she turn around?"

"Her cell phone." Cade said it at the same time as Laurel spotted it on top of the TV.

"She got up to answer her cell phone." Her stomach sank to the floor. "It was me. I called her from the airport at that very moment."

"Your call may have saved her life."

Laurel frowned at him.

"If she'd been sitting on the couch, the attacker would have had a much better angle, and the blow would have struck much harder. It could have killed her."

Laurel looked at the cell phone. "Have you got gloves?"

"Nope. You'll have to use a tissue."

"Misty assured me she'd be at home. She always watches *Secret Lives* at six. At first I thought she didn't answer because she was engrossed in the show." She pulled a couple of tissues from a box on the end table and used them to pick up Misty's phone. She accessed the incoming calls.

"I called her at 6:25 when the plane landed. Then at

6:58, and 7:20." She looked at the muted TV. The logo in the corner of the screen identified the station that carried *Secret Lives.* "If she was watching the show, then she was attacked after it started but before it ended. So she was attacked between 6:00 and 6:30."

As soon as she'd seen Misty's floor littered with photos and paper, she'd known what the attacker was after. But now she had to face her own responsibility for Misty's attack. Her mouth tasted like cotton. She couldn't delay any longer. No matter what Cade thought of her shaky theory, she had to come clean. She needed his help.

"So you think my phone call kept her from being hurt even *worse.* I suppose that's some comfort, considering—" She stopped. This was as hard as she'd known it would be.

His intense blue eyes held hers, lasering holes in her confidence. "Considering what?"

She didn't know if he was reacting to the guilt that must be written all over her face or the sudden tension that tightened like springs through her entire body, but his demeanor changed.

He uncrossed his arms and casually flexed his fingers near the pocket of his sweats. At the same time he shifted his weight to the balls of his feet. He was poised and ready for anything. The transformation was an awesome and frightening sight.

"Do you see what's all over the floor? Photos. Scrapbooks. Journals." She gestured toward the hardwood floor. "I know why Misty was attacked."

Cade didn't speak, nor did he move his hand.

"All this—" this time she included the bloodstain on the floor and the couch in her sweeping gesture "—is my fault."

Chapter Two

Cade Dupree didn't know what it was about Laurel Gillespie, but he was having a devil of a time taking his eyes off her. If it hadn't been for one glaring incident back in high school, he wouldn't even have remembered her. She'd been a year behind him and two years behind his brother. His memory of her was of braces and glasses and wildly curly red hair.

The reason he remembered that much was because of the part his brother James had played in embarrassing her in front of the whole school.

She'd changed. Now her dark red hair was pulled back into a loose braid, but it still wasn't totally tamed. Wisps and waves floated around her face. Unobscured by braces and glasses, her delicate features were lovely.

Yep. She'd changed a *lot*.

"Cade, I want to get to the hospital and check on Misty. She's going to be scared to death when she realizes where she is."

Cade took off his baseball cap, folded the brim and stuck it into his back pocket. "Five seconds ago I'd have said go ahead, but you just inserted yourself into the middle of this. You want to explain why this is your fault?" He leaned against the door facing and crossed his arms.

To his surprise, her face turned pink.

"I got an invitation to our ten-year high school reunion, but I hated high school. I never intended to come back to town. But Misty begged me to come. I told her I'd think about it."

Cade blew out an impatient breath.

"This is relevant, *Chief Dupree.* I was going to wait a day or two and call her back with an excuse. In the meantime, I pulled out snapshots from high school— mostly of graduation night. I wanted to review faces and names." She turned back toward him and reached into her jacket pocket.

Instinctively, he tensed. It was a ridiculous reaction, totally at odds with her words and body language.

"I found something."

He flexed his fingers as she pulled out a small stack of snapshots. She held them out.

He took them and shuffled through them. "Yeah? What?"

"Something that would never happen in a million years."

He frowned at her but she just leveled a gaze at him. He stepped over to a small desk and turned on a lamp. He scrutinized the photos under the bright light. They were mostly snapshots of Laurel and Misty.

The two girls wore white dresses and held their caps and gowns. Both were grinning from ear to ear. Cade studied the awkward high-school Laurel. She wore a dress that hung on her like a sack. Her delicate bone structure and pretty features were not quite obscured by those ugly glasses and braces.

If he or any other guy had bothered to really look at her, they'd have seen what he saw now. Little skinny carrottop Laurel had been destined to be a knockout.

"Put the photos side by side."

"You could just tell me, you know." He laid them out like a game of solitaire, then leaned over to study them more closely.

"Back then, I didn't notice anything odd in the photos, but looking at them now, with seven years of experience in criminology under my belt, what I see doesn't add up."

"Who are these people?" He pointed. "I recognize Misty and you. Nice braces."

She sniffed.

"Who's that standing behind you two?"

She stepped closer and Cade got a whiff of the scent of gardenias floating around her.

"That's Wendell Vance."

"Vance? Where do I know that name?"

"He died that night."

A vague memory surfaced. "He hanged himself."

Her nod stirred the air near his cheek. He picked up one of the photos and looked at it more closely under the light.

"Notice anything odd?"

"No. I barely remember him."

"Look at his face."

"Okay. His face is red. Embarrassed?"

"You don't remember what happened that night? What the CeeGees did?"

He shook his head. He'd been at Ole Miss when Laurel's class graduated. "The CeeGees?"

"The Cool Girls. You know, Debra Evans, Kathy Hodges, Mary Sue Nelson and Sheryl Posey. Their mission in life was to prey on shy girls and geeky boys."

The girls who'd played the prank on her.

"They taped a sign to his back during graduation that said *Wendell Vance has a pencil in his pants.*"

"Ouch." He suppressed a grin—almost.

"It's not funny." Her hazel eyes sparked.

"Yeah. It is."

She propped her fists on her hips. "They humiliated him in front of his parents, his teachers, his classmates."

He nodded. "I remember Dad talking about it. He thought that was the reason Wendell killed himself."

"So did everybody. But look here." Laurel tapped the snapshot with a trimmed manicured nail.

He squinted. "A girl's hand on his shoulder. So?"

"Not just any girl's hand. That's—"

"Cade!"

Laurel jumped. Cade looked toward the door. *Oh, damn.* It was Debra, Fred Evans's daughter.

"Dad told me something happened to Misty. What is it? Can I do anything to help?" Her eyes darted around the room and came to rest on the blood in front of the couch.

"Oh, my God!" She turned white as a sheet, then scurried into the room, a plump hand covering her mouth. "I think I may throw up."

Laurel eyed her. Interesting that she had rushed *toward* the bloodstain as she threatened to throw up. But then Debra had always been a bit of a drama queen. Based on how she was acting, Laurel would wager that the former CeeGee knew exactly what she would find in Misty's living room. The only thing that wasn't fake was her pallor.

In two long strides, Cade reached Debra's side. "Deb, your dad's a police officer. You know better than to cross crime-scene tape."

"But—why would anyone hurt Misty? Was it a burglary?" She turned and spotted Laurel. "Who—?"

Laurel saw the blank look on Debra's face. She'd

expected it—she looked a lot different without braces and thick glasses. Still, it sent that ridiculous knee-jerk reaction through her—disappointment that someone who'd known her didn't recognize her. She thought she'd left those high-school insecurities far behind.

"I'm Laurel Gillespie, Debra."

"Laurel? Oh, Laurel *Gillespie.* So you're not married yet? I guess you're here for the reunion?"

Laurel nodded.

Debra turned to Cade. "Why does she get to be here?"

Cade stepped closer. "Because she's an FBI special agent."

Debra's face drained of color again. "FBI? Cade, oh, my God. Did you call in the FBI?"

Cade put his hand on the small of Debra's back and guided her toward the door. She smiled up at him and put her arm around his waist.

Laurel clamped her jaw. This wasn't high school. So why was she letting these small-town divas get to her?

Just as Cade guided Debra into the foyer, she glanced back at Laurel. For a microsecond her eyes narrowed and dropped to the photographs in Laurel's hand. Then she looked her straight in the eye. Laurel saw something in her gaze—something she couldn't put her finger on.

She was sure of one thing, though. Debra wasn't as shocked and faint as she pretended to be.

Cade came back in, shaking his head. "There are still a few folks outside, watching the house like vultures. This is the biggest crime Dusty Springs has seen since old man Rabb shot his son-in-law in the butt."

He walked over to her. "You were telling me why this is all your fault."

"We were talking about what the CeeGees did to Wendell on graduation night."

"You think this is all about a silly high-school clique from ten years ago? What's the big deal?"

"The big deal is that they didn't care who they hurt. They ridiculed Wendell Vance on the most important night of his life. When he walked across that stage to accept the Science Medal—the school's most prestigious award, nobody applauded. Everybody laughed. It was horrible." She felt tears prick her eyes. "Then the next morning—"

"It was discovered that he'd hanged himself down by the creek using the old rope swing. What does that have to do with this?"

"It's in the photo. The hand on Wendell's shoulder. Look really close."

He held the photos directly under the lamp. "Okay. I see the hand. Could we stop playing twenty questions?"

"That hand belongs to one of the CeeGees."

"How do you know?"

"See the ring. Kathy had them made special for herself and the other girls."

"I still don't get it. So she's making a big deal over Wendell. So what?"

She spread her hands. "If a CeeGee was flirting with a guy like Wendell, then it had to be because they weren't through with him. They were planning something else that night."

"You really resent them, don't you?"

"This is not about me. It's about what happened to Wendell."

"What? What happened to Wendell? Besides the fact that he was obviously a troubled kid. I don't get your point. You said what you saw in the photo didn't add up."

Laurel blew out a frustrated breath. "That's right. I can't shake the feeling that this photo is telling us something important. Think about it. Wendell got the Science Medal. It carried a ten-thousand-dollar scholarship with it. I remember wishing I could win it, but by the beginning of our senior year it was obvious that it was a two-man race— Wendell Vance and Ralph Langston."

"Ten grand. I didn't realize that."

She nodded. "Wendell had been accepted at Vanderbilt. With all that ahead of him, why would he kill himself?"

"Maybe he couldn't take the humiliation of what they did to him."

"That's not enough."

"Kids kill themselves because they get turned down for a date. It's sad but true."

Laurel heard the doubt in his voice. Her frustration grew. She knew her theory was shaky.

Shaky? It was barely more than a niggle of intuition fed by a couple of odd occurrences. Cade was about two seconds away from dismissing her as a conspiracy theorist.

"The more I looked at this photo, the more sure I was that this went beyond a kid hanging himself because somebody pulled a prank on him. I had to come back here and at least see if I could unearth anything about his death."

Cade pushed his fingers through his hair, and then rubbed the back of his neck. "Wow. As theories go, yours is pretty thin."

"I know. That's why I called and asked Misty to pull out her photos. But I screwed up. I should have made sure she was alone before I started talking." She spread her hands. "She was in the middle of a Reunion Planning Committee meeting. Everybody in the room overheard her talking about Wendell and the graduation night photos. I tried to stop the conversation once I realized she had company, but it was too late."

Cade looked at his watch. "I don't get what you're driving at."

"You know who's on the Reunion Planning Committee?"

"Sure. Ann Noble from the Mayor's office, Ralph Langston, Kathy Adler, Debra Honeycutt and—" he paused for an instant "—and Mary Sue Nelson."

"Right. Three of the CeeGees. It was one of them who attacked Misty."

"How do you figure?"

Laurel looked at Cade's solemn face. Would he believe her? He had to. Without his help she didn't have a prayer of uncovering the truth.

"Those three snapshots are the only ones I had that caught Wendell in them. And none of them show the CeeGee's face. I was hoping Misty had a shot that revealed more."

Cade's gaze sharpened. "You're thinking Misty's attacker was after her photos."

Laurel steeled herself against Cade's possible ridicule. "Yes. I think the owner of that hand was planning a bigger humiliation for Wendell than a rude sign on his back." She tapped the photo with her fingernail. "A CeeGee would never go near a geek like Wendell. I'm afraid Wendell didn't commit suicide. I think when we find out whose hand that is, we'll find Wendell's murderer."

LAUREL'S WORDS stunned Cade. He was still chewing on her theory that Wendell Vance might have been murdered when they got to Three Springs Hospital. He understood what Laurel was getting at, but it was a damn big stretch to go from a flirtation captured by a photo to homicide.

Misty Waller was in an emergency room cubicle. Her pretty, round face was almost as pale as the bandage on her head. The skin around her closed eyes was a faint purple. She was going to end up with a couple of shiners.

"I'm so sorry," Laurel said, squeezing Misty's hand. "This is my fault."

Cade leaned against the wall with his arms crossed. Laurel had asked him to let her talk to Misty first. He didn't like it, but he couldn't think of a good reason to say no. Misty might tell her more than she'd tell him.

"Don't be silly. You couldn't know someone would break into my—" Misty's voice cracked and she lifted a trembling hand to touch the bandage on her head. She turned her pale blue eyes toward Cade. "I can't stay here, Cade. Make them let me go home. My cat—my house—"

Cade caught Laurel's eye. Misty's voice was too high. She was on the verge of hysteria.

"We'll get you home just as soon as the doctors tell us we can," Laurel said, patting Misty's arm. "But right now, I need to know what happened. Everything you can remember."

Misty closed her eyes and licked her lips. "I don't remember anything. Can you call the doctor now? I have to get home."

"He'll be here in a few minutes," Laurel said gently. "Did the nurse give you something?"

Without opening her eyes, Misty nodded. "She said it would calm me down but it's not working."

Laurel met Cade's gaze. "It will. Just give it time. You had a shock. What you were doing this afternoon?"

"While I waited to hear from you, I finished transcribing a stack of depositions for the law firm I work for. Then I turned up the sound on the TV and watched the latest episode of *Secret Lives.*"

Cade stepped closer. "You turned up the sound? When did you turn it back down?"

Misty frowned up at him. "I didn't. At least I don't think I did."

If Misty hadn't turned the sound down, that explained why she didn't hear the attacker. But why was the sound off when Laurel got there? He made a brief note to double-check the prints on the TV.

"So watching *Secret Lives* is the last thing you remember? What about your high-school pictures? Did you find them?" Laurel asked.

"Yes." Misty smiled wanly. "I was looking at them this morning. I can't believe what we looked like. Oh, jiminy, Laurel. We were so skinny."

Laurel laughed softly. "And we were always dieting. And then running out at midnight for ice cream."

Misty nodded and winced.

Enough reminiscing. Cade stepped forward, but Laurel held up a hand.

He clenched his jaw. Did she think he was going to sit back and let her run this case? She might be an FBI agent, but she couldn't do anything unless he officially asked for the Bureau's help.

His granddad had been chief of police in Dusty Springs before his dad. And although everyone had expected Cade's brother James to take over the job, now it was *his*. He was the law in town and he knew how to handle a crime. He didn't need a big-city FBI agent to do his job for him.

The two women laughed. One laugh was high and tinkly, like broken glass. The other, Laurel's, was low, throaty, sexy. A thrill of pure lust streaked through him, surprising him.

Down boy. This wasn't the time or the place. He shifted his weight and tried to keep his expression neutral. Even if it had been a long time since he'd been so strongly and immediately attracted to a woman.

He concentrated on Misty. At least Laurel had managed to calm her down.

That was her intent, he realized suddenly. Still—*two minutes.* No more. Then he was going to step in and ask the important questions.

"Did you find any pictures from graduation night?" Laurel asked.

"I found some in one of the photo boxes. I haven't had a chance to look at them, though."

"Where's the box?"

"I put it back."

Laurel smiled. "That's right. You always put everything back. I never did. Misty, remember when I called the other day and you told me you were in a meeting?"

Cade's irritation fizzled and his opinion of her skills raised a notch. She'd gone from caring friend to FBI agent inside of a minute, and he'd barely noticed the transition. He was certain Misty hadn't.

"Sure." Misty's drooping eyes opened. "A Reunion Committee Meeting at my house."

"Who all was there?" Cade broke in. He knew who was on the committee, but not who had attended that meeting.

Misty squinted at him. "Kathy of course. And her minions." She cut her eyes over to Laurel, who laughed softly.

"Debra and Mary Sue. And Sheryl," Laurel supplied.

"Not Sheryl. I haven't seen her in years."

"Who else?" Cade asked.

She closed her eyes again. "Ann Noble. And Ralph Langston. He's funding the whole shebang."

The curtain around the emergency room cubicle fluttered and a nurse stuck her head in. "Ms. Waller, Dr. Cook wants a CT scan of your head, just to be sure you're okay." She stepped over to the gurney and patted one of the pillows. "And he wants you to stay overnight, so we can watch you."

Misty's calm evaporated and her eyes grew wide and panicky. "No, I can't stay here. Please. Where's the doctor—"

"I'll stay with you," Laurel said. "Don't worry."

"The technician will be here in a few minutes to take you to the lab," the nurse said, then left.

"Oh, Laurel, thank you. But I'm more worried about Harriet. She'll be so scared in that house alone."

"Harriet?"

"Harriet Potter. My kitten. She was Harry until I realized she was a girl."

"Don't worry," Laurel said. "I'll take care of her." As she leaned over and kissed Misty on the forehead, Cade's gaze zeroed in on her curvy backside. Her jacket rode up and he saw the tip of the leather paddle holster at the small of her back.

Something went haywire inside him at the sight of her weapon. He suddenly had to hold his breath and avert his gaze. He shifted his stance to try and hide an embarrassing truth. The sight of Laurel's Glock holstered at the small of her back was a huge turn-on. Which surprised the hell out of him. He'd never thought of a woman with a gun as sexy before. In fact, he'd always thought those women-in-black-kicking-butt TV shows were a little silly. Maybe he'd have to give them another chance.

Laurel patted Misty's hair and straightened. Misty gave her a tiny smile and her eyes grew damp at the corners. "Thank you. It's so good to see you."

"It's good to see you, too."

Cade felt like a fifth wheel. He wasn't much for tearful reunions or sappy reminiscences. He was a lot more comfortable behind his badge.

He cleared his throat. "We'd better go, Agent Gillespie."

Laurel's head snapped up and her hazel eyes sparked. She got his message.

"I'll be back first thing in the morning," she said to Misty. "I'm sure by then they'll be ready to let you go home."

She stood just as Mary Sue Nelson breezed in, carrying a funeral-size vase of flowers.

"Misty, darling! What in the world happened? Did you fall down the steps or something?"

"Hi, Mary Sue. Somebody attacked me," Misty said groggily.

Mary Sue looked at her quizzically before she turned toward Cade.

"Hello, Cade. What are you doing here? Was she really attacked? Who could have done that?" She giggled.

Cade had to make himself relax his jaw. "Hi, Mary Sue." He could see it now. The scene at Misty's house was nothing. By the time Misty was admitted there would be a constant stream of concerned neighbors parading in and out of her hospital room. It was the small-town way.

"I tell you what," he said. "They're coming to get Misty for a CT scan in a couple of minutes. Why don't we all get out of here and let her rest for a while?"

"Cade Dupree, you may be police chief, but my mom babysat you when you were in diapers. So watch who you're giving orders to." Mary Sue batted her eyelashes at him and laid her fingers on his arm.

Laurel met his gaze, her eyes sparkling dangerously.

Uh oh.

"Here, Mary Sue," Laurel said. "Let me put that *glorious* bouquet over here. Where in the world did you get that at this time of night? Now you can have *both* hands free to talk to Cade." She took the vase from Mary Sue's hands. "There. I could hardly see you behind all the flowers."

"Do I know you?"

"I'm Laurel Gillespie."

Mary Sue didn't even acknowledge her. She turned back to Cade. "Who do you think attacked Misty? Was it a gang?"

The nurse returned with an aide who unlocked the gurney's wheels and began to maneuver it toward the door.

"You should all go home now. Once they've done her CT scan, they'll put her in a room overnight." She eyed each one of them in turn. "Visiting hours start at 9:00 a.m."

Mary Sue waggled her fingers at Misty, then turned to Cade. "My husband's out of town. I'm not sure it's safe for me to be home alone."

"I'm sure you'll be fine. If you're worried, you could go *across the street* to your mother's," Cade replied.

He felt Laurel's eyes boring into his back and he knew he was in for it. Sure enough, as soon as Mary Sue left, Laurel placed her hand on his arm.

"Why Mister Dupree," she drawled. "Are you certain it's safe for me out there alone?"

He should have been irritated, should have shrugged off her hand as soon as she touched him. But her fingers on his forearm felt so different from Mary Sue's. Mary Sue's touch had been clingy, needy. Laurel's was firm and enticing.

He cleared his throat and pulled his arm away. "Knock it off, *Special Agent* Gillespie."

"I got your point the first time," she whispered. "This isn't old home-week. I'm a professional, *Chief* Dupree. I know we're investigating a crime."

"We?" *No way.* She was a witness, but that was all. He held the curtain for her to exit the cubicle ahead of him and didn't say anything more until they reached the parking lot.

Laurel turned to him as they approached his pickup.

"Tell me about Ralph Langston. How is he funding the whole reunion?"

"He moved back here about a year ago," Cade said. "He bought all that land down by the creek, and broke ground for a state-of-the-art convention complex."

"So Ralph made it big?"

"Yes, he owns the fifth largest web-hosting company on the Internet. And he developed Webelot, the Web page building software."

"Wow."

"He's hosting the reunion at the Visitor Center, and he's footing the bill."

"Visitor Center?"

"Right. On the rise above the creek bank, where the old high school burned."

She looked at him, her expression thoughtful. "I want to go down there."

"What for? You'll see it tomorrow night. That's where the party's going to be."

"Not the Visitor Center. The creek bank. Where Wendell died."

He opened the passenger door of his pickup, but as she started to get in, he stopped her with a touch on her elbow. "This is not your case. It's mine. You're on vacation. Remember?"

Laurel stiffened and lifted her chin until her nose was only a few inches from his. "I found Misty. I know what her attacker was looking for. I just gave you a roomful of suspects. Of course it's my case, too."

"You're a witness. Nothing more."

"You could request the help of the FBI."

"I don't think so. All we have here is a home invasion and assault. Nothing the FBI deals with."

She closed the distance between them by an inch. "What we have here is an unsolved mystery. I work in the Unsolved Mysteries Division of the FBI."

"There is absolutely no evidence that Wendell Vance's death was anything more than a suicide."

"Yes, there is—somewhere. Whoever attacked Misty was after her pictures. That's obvious. They were trying to destroy evidence. But I intend to find it first." Her chin went a bit higher, and he could feel her warm breath on his lips.

His whole body went on red alert. *Danger!*

Gardenias. Warm, sweet breath. A cute little nose and now that he was close enough to see them—freckles.

His thighs tightened. Heat spread through his groin and radiated outward. In a few seconds he was going to have a huge hard-on. What the hell kind of Police Chief got hot and bothered by a *witness?*

A sarcastic voice in his head answered him. *A horny one.*

"Nope. I'm involved," Laurel continued. "You said it yourself, Dupree. I inserted myself into this case."

"Yeah," he heard the strain in his voice. "You sure did." He took a step backward, out of harm's way—for the moment. He knew she was right. He was going to have to work with her. But this crazy physical attraction had to stop.

It must be because he hadn't had sex in such a long time. Man, he didn't even want to think about how long it had been.

His body chose that instant to remind him just how deprived it was feeling. He took another step backward and pretended he couldn't still smell gardenias or see her freckles.

When she sat, her skirt rode up to her thighs. Despite his irrational anger, his mouth went dry and his libido spiraled out of control. He slammed the door with a vengeance it didn't deserve and stalked around to the driver's side.

When he got in, Laurel grabbed his arm. "Cade, I just remembered something."

He wished she'd quit touching him, and while she was at it, quit wafting that gardenia perfume his way. Everything about her was playing havoc with his good sense. He looked down at her hand then up at her. "Yeah?"

"Ralph Langston got the ten-thousand-dollar scholarship after Wendell died."

Chapter Three

Later that evening, when Cade came out of the shower, his phone was ringing. A glance at the caller ID told him it was his dad. He picked up the handset.

"Dad, I was going to call you in the morning. What are you doing up at this hour?"

"I wanted to check on you. Gotta keep up with the only son I've got left."

Cade rubbed his chest. The pain was old and familiar, but still sharp. *Only son I have left.* That's how his dad always referred to him. As if he was nothing but James's leftovers.

His brother, James Dupree Senior's first-born, had died five years before. The same week his dad had suffered a stroke that had left him with a mild speech impediment. Every time Cade talked to him, he was reminded of both.

"We had a breaking-and-entering at Misty Waller's house."

"I heard. Misty okay?"

"She's got a knot on her head, but she's fine." Cade paused, glancing at the clock. "Dad, feel like talking for a minute?"

"It's why I called."

"What do you remember about Wendell Vance's death?" Cade paced as he talked.

"Vance? Oh. Kid that hanged himself on his graduation night?"

"Right." His dad might have trouble speaking, but there was nothing wrong with his brain.

"Ever'thin's in the file, I reckon."

"Did you ever think it was murder?"

"Murder? Maybe for a minute. Remember what I tol' you? Always consider every possibility. But the boy was taking pills for depression. It's all in the file."

"What did you think about Ralph Langston?"

"Who?"

"He was in the same class. Apparently he got a ten-thousand-dollar scholarship that would have gone to Wendell."

"Don' remember that. I musta talked to him. Everybody was all shook up. I gotta say though, the boy did a good job of killin' himself—"

"Good job? What do you mean?" Cade pushed his fingers through his damp hair, raining cool drops of water onto his shoulders and back.

"He tied that rope that hangs from the Swinging Oak 'round his neck. Broke his hyoid bone and crushed his larynx. Quickes' way. Beats choking slow."

"Hyoid bone." Cade thought back to his forensics training from Quantico. "That doesn't usually happen in a hanging, does it?"

"Nah. Only thing I could figure was maybe that disk an' chain got caught in the rope."

"Disk? Oh—the Science Medal. He was still wearing it when he hanged himself?" The metal disk could have gotten caught between the rope and Wendell's throat, crushing the bone.

"That was strange, too," his dad continued. "Never did

find that medal. Just a coupla links of chain. If I didn' know better, I'd say somebody took it."

Cade stopped pacing. "Could it have fallen into the creek?"

"I wondered about that. But the pieces of chain I found were about six feet or so to the left of the body."

Cade wiped his face with the towel. "Left. Not in front, not behind."

"That's right. Odd."

"What did you do with it?"

"It's in the evidence room with the case file. We looked for that medal for days. Your brother helped. That was the week he told me he was droppin' out of college and joinin' the service." Emotion choked his dad's voice.

Cade's chest squeezed tighter. He rubbed it again, his palm spreading the few drops of water that clung. He hadn't remembered James helping Dad with the investigation of Wendell Vance's death. Was there anything his brother *hadn't* done before him?

Cade sighed. "It's been a long day, Dad. I'd better let you get to bed. I'll see you in a day or two, okay?"

"Sure. Cade?"

"Yeah?"

"You thinkin' the Vance boy was murdered? Why now?"

"This weekend's the ten year reunion of his high school class. People are talking."

"This have anythin' to do with Misty's attack?"

"Maybe. I'm checking into it."

"Take care, son."

"I will. Good night, Dad."

Cade hung up and flopped down onto his unmade bed. He stared at the ceiling and thought about what his dad had said.

He was impressed with his dad's memory of the case and the thoroughness of his investigation.

He punched a pillow and doubled it up under his head. Tomorrow he'd pull out Wendell Vance's old case files and go over them. He'd meant to ask his dad if he'd dusted the links of chain for prints, but he'd find the answer to that in the file.

He could already hear Laurel when she found out Wendell's cause of death. A broken hyoid usually indicated foul play. Her criminologist brain would go straight to murder. He wondered if he could hold her back for two days, until the reunion was over.

There was no way he'd let her whip the town into a frenzy by spouting her theories of murder. Hell, they were based on nothing—just a few odd photos.

She would disagree of course. He could see her now, with those wisps of red hair framing her angry face and her multicolored eyes flashing.

He'd learned one thing about her tonight. Laurel Gillespie didn't like to be wrong.

His thoughts drifted to his first view of her behind in that tight gray skirt. What a surprise she was. He'd barely remembered her from high school. And only because of his brother's involvement in the prank the—what had she called them—the *CeeGees* had played on her. James, arrogant and assured, had thought it was hilarious.

A pang of compassion for Laurel and the CeeGees's other victims pricked his conscience. He hadn't been involved, but could he have stopped James if he'd tried? He doubted it.

At least Laurel hadn't let their cruel jokes wreck her life. She was in the FBI—and not just a field agent. She worked for an elite division stationed in D.C.

He punched his pillow again, then stuffed it back under his neck. He'd dreamed of being an FBI agent once, before James had died.

Even in death, his brother had bested him. All his life, Cade had worshiped James. He'd wanted to be just like him.

James should have been the one to take over the job of police chief in Dusty Springs. But instead, he'd joined the Air Force. Then, within five years, he was gone. And as his dad had just said, Cade was the only son he had left.

So when his dad had his stroke, Cade had come home to Dusty Springs. Now here he was five years later, Chief of Police just like his dad and granddad, and still angry at his brother for dying.

Cade knew the job he was doing was honorable and important, but he'd never intended to stay in Dusty Springs, where he'd always be in the shadow of his brother. After he'd returned, it had gotten even worse. It was hard enough to live up to a shining star like James. But it was impossible when the star was a hero who'd given his life for his country.

He uttered a short laugh. Just went to show how different real life was from high school. He'd been determined to outdo James. And he'd come close. In the high school yearbook, guys like him were *Most Likely to Succeed* or *Most Popular* or *Mr. Dusty Springs High School*—all those accolades that were so important back then.

Laurel, on the other hand, would be found in a group photo of the choir, or as a member of the Home Economics Club.

Strange how things turned out.

An odd sensation cramped his chest. Was he *jealous* of her success in the Bureau? Or even more so because she'd managed to leave Dusty Springs behind?

Nah. He just needed some sleep. Turning over, he pulled the sheet over him. In the morning, he'd dig out Wendell Vance's old file. It couldn't hurt to see if Laurel's theory held any merit.

LAUREL WAS CAUGHT *in traffic on the beltway. Car horns blared all around her. She was late already and now more cars were honking.*

She jerked awake and met a slanted green gaze. Her heart slammed into her throat. "Eek! Cat."

The feline hissed and jumped over her and off the bed. Her brain instantly processed her surroundings. Cat. Canopied bed. Misty's house.

"Ssss yourself, Harriet. You scared me!"

Undaunted, Harriet leapt onto the foot of the bed and curled up on top of the covers.

The car horn still blared. It wasn't just in her dream. It sounded like it was right outside the house. Her rental car?

She sighed, glancing at the clock. It was 3:00 a.m. Of course it was her car.

She got up and slid her feet into thong sandals. By habit, she grabbed her weapon and her car keys on her way out.

As soon as she opened the front door, she saw the rental car's emergency lights blinking. She ran out, unlocked the car door, jumped into the driver's seat and deactivated the alarm. Once it was quiet, she sat there for a moment, looking up and down the street.

The night was moonless, and the streetlights gave off very little illumination.

Nothing. Not even a fluttering curtain. After the excitement earlier, she couldn't believe no one had stuck their head out to see what the noise was. Still, car alarms went off all the time, probably even in Dusty Springs.

But something must have triggered it. Had someone tried to break into her car?

After a few seconds, she got out and inspected the vehicle. There were no scrapes or dents. No sign of force on the windows or doors. Maybe a kid had tried the door to see if it was unlocked.

With a last look around the deserted street, she walked back up the steps to the house. She opened the door cautiously, watching to be sure she didn't let the cat out.

Just as she closed the door behind her, a blast of cold stinging spray hit her in the face. Surprise and burning pain streaked through her like lightning.

After a split second's shock, she ducked and rolled but it was too late. She'd been maced. Her face burned like fire. Her eyes wouldn't open. The pain was agonizing.

Then a blanket was thrown over her head and a shoe kicked her in the ribs. She curled into a fetal position. It was all she could do. She was blinded by the Mace.

Her attacker kicked her again, this time in the kidney. She grunted. Then the front door opened and slammed.

Laurel fought the suffocating blanket. She finally got it off her. Pulling herself up to her hands and knees she felt for her weapon. It was gone. She crawled blindly toward the bathroom, feeling around the hardwood floor. The gun must have slid farther than she'd thought.

Finally, her fingers encountered cold ceramic tile. Her eyes leaked tears, even though she had them squeezed tightly shut. She crawled to the bathtub and felt for the cold water faucet.

Taking a deep breath, she splashed her face. The water made everything burn twice as badly, but it eventually washed away the sticky pepper spray.

Laurel leaned over the tub and kept sluicing her face and eyes. After what seemed like hours, the pain lessened to a manageable level.

She sat on the floor, her chest heaving with huge sobs. But there was no time to indulge herself. She had to find her Glock. If whoever had attacked her had taken it—alarm squeezed her chest like a giant fist.

She pulled herself up using a towel rack. She was wobbly, and her eyes still burned. She felt her way out of the bathroom, alert to any sound. She'd thought she'd heard the front door slam, but she'd been in such pain she couldn't be sure.

The intruder might still be inside the house.

She took a deep breath and coughed. Did she smell smoke, or was the Mace affecting her sense of smell? Forcing her eyes open, she saw a red, flickering glow coming from the den.

Fire! She lunged for the door. She rounded the frame and met the flames engulfing the dining room tabletop. They licked at the drapes.

"No!" Laurel cried. Misty's pictures! She had to stop it. But before she could move, the drapes caught. In an instant the ancient fabric was swallowed up by flames and a tongue of fire licked out toward a damask-covered easy chair.

Helpless against the fast-growing inferno, she backed away from the rising heat. She had to call the fire department.

But her cell phone was back in the bedroom in her jacket pocket. She never had her damn phone when she needed it. She turned and headed for the door and ran into a hard body. Her instincts took over and she doubled her fists. She swung as hard as she could.

"No!" she yelled. "No!"

"LAUREL, IT'S ME, Cade." Cade dodged Laurel's fists and pinned her arms. He whirled and thrust her toward the front door, his brain registering relief that she seemed unhurt.

"Stay on the porch," he shouted, tossing her his phone. "Press 8. Fire department."

Then he ran up the hall to the kitchen. Where did Misty keep her fire extinguisher? He glanced quickly around the old-fashioned kitchen. Nothing. He opened the cabinets under the sink. There—in the back.

Grabbing it, praying it worked, he headed for the den.

Half the room was engulfed in flames, and the heat was nearly unbearable. He sprayed, but the little fire extinguisher wasn't up to such a big job.

Just as he had emptied the canister, he heard the sirens. The advancing flames forced him out of the room.

Laurel stood on the porch holding his cell phone in one hand and Misty's cat in the other. The cat was squirming and yowling.

"You can let her down. She'll be okay," Cade said.

Laurel let go and Harriet took off into the darkness.

"What about you? Are you hurt?"

She shook her head jerkily and he put his arm around her waist and led her down the steps into the yard.

"What happened?" he started, but the arrival of the fire truck interrupted him.

He pulled her out of the way as the town's volunteer firemen rushed inside with the fire hose. The roar of pressurized water drowned out the roar of the fire. Within a few minutes, the fire was out.

But as Cade knew from experience, the excitement was far from over. He enlisted his patrolman Fred Evans, who'd shown up with his hair sticking straight out in back, to maintain crowd control and told him to call Officer Shelton Phillips.

If possible, there were more people milling around than a few hours earlier when Misty was hurt. He answered the same questions at least two dozen times.

No, no one was hurt.

Yes, it was odd that Misty was attacked and her house burned on the same night.

No, he didn't have any leads.

No, he didn't need any help pulling sodden furniture or charred items out of the house.

Yes, it *would* help if everyone would just go on home to bed.

Finally, Fred and a couple of other men managed to disperse the crowd and Cade went to speak with Kit Haydel, the fire chief.

"That could have been a bad one," Kit said, pulling off his gloves. "I wish people would get rid of all the fire hazards in these old houses." He wiped his forehead with his forearm. "Bad wiring, rotting fabric and dried-out wood all over the place."

"But bad wiring didn't cause this fire."

Kit shook his head. "There was a stack of papers and photo albums in the middle of the dining room table. Preliminary investigation indicates that the fire started there. And it wasn't an accident."

Cade nodded. "I figured that. How do you know?"

"It's an amateur setup. The smell of lighter fluid is all over the place."

"I didn't smell anything but smoke."

Kit grinned. "You work enough fires, you eventually learn the different smells. Lighter fluid's different than electrical or gasoline or a cigarette."

One of the firemen hollered at Kit, who waved at him.

"How'd you get here so fast?" he asked Cade.

"I heard the car alarm, and since we'd already had one situation tonight, I thought I'd better check it out."

"Car alarm?"

Cade frowned. "Didn't you hear it? Your house is about as close to Misty's as mine is."

"I was asleep."

Cade had been, too—he'd thought. But when the faint sound of the car alarm had reached his ears, he'd immediately thought of Laurel.

"Need me for anything else tonight, Cade?"

"God, I hope not. We've had plenty of excitement for one day." He nodded toward the house. "Can I get inside? Check for damage and evidence?"

"Yeah. I think we got all the hot spots."

"Great. Thanks. You'll get me a copy of your report, right?"

Kit sent him a mock salute as he climbed onto the fire truck.

Cade looked around. Thank goodness the rubberneckers had dispersed. Over by their cars, Fred and Shelton stood talking with a couple of neighbors. Every so often, one of them would gesture or point toward the house.

He didn't see anyone else. A tremor of alarm streaked through him. He stalked over to Fred. "Where'd Laurel go?"

Fred frowned and glanced at Shelton, who shook his head. "Haven't seen her since the firemen got here."

"She must have gone back inside. Thanks, guys." Cade sprinted toward the house.

"Hey, you want some help?" Fred called.

"Nope. Y'all head on home."

He took the front steps two at a time and burst through the front door. The smell of wet, charred wood and fabric permeated the house.

He heard a cough coming from the den.

Laurel was standing just inside the door, facing the sodden mess that had been her friend's living room. Her arms were folded and her fingers were white-knuckled.

"You shouldn't be in here."

She shrugged without turning around. "Where else should I be? Look what they did. Misty will be devastated."

He took her arm and turned her around. "You need to— God, Laurel. What happened to you?"

Her face was red and her eyes were nearly swollen shut. He grabbed her other arm and squinted at her in the pale light shining in from the street lamps. "Were you burned? Why didn't you tell me?"

She shook her head. "No. The fire was after."

"After what? What are you talking about?"

He studied her more closely. Only her face was red. Her bare arms and shoulders were as smooth and peachy-pink as he remembered them.

And she was soaking wet. He slid his palms up her arms, feeling her skin shiver at his touch. He clenched his jaw and dragged his gaze back to her face. "Tell me, Laurel. What's wrong with your face—your eyes?"

She wrapped her arms around herself. "Is everyone gone? I really don't want the whole town to know what happened. We need to keep this information quiet."

He frowned at her. Her voice didn't go with her words. The words were those of an investigator working a crime scene. Her voice, however, was small and scared.

He walked over to the window and peered outside. Everyone had gone. There were no cars on the street except for his and hers. A couple of houses down, where Kathy Adler lived, a light went off as he watched.

He turned back to Laurel. "They're all gone. Now tell me what happened here."

She kept her eyes closed while she talked. "My car alarm went off a little while ago and I ran out to reset it." She rubbed her temple. "As soon as I stepped back inside the house, I was blasted with pepper spray. I went down."

Alarm arrowed through him. "*Inside* the house?"

She nodded. "They threw me down in the hall, tossed a blanket over my head and kicked me. Then I heard the front door slam. I can't believe I didn't see them when I went out."

"Obviously whoever it was hid in the shadows," Cade said as he wrapped his fingers around her upper arm. "Come here. I want to see your face."

"It's okay. I need to put more cold water on it."

He pulled out a mini-flashlight and shone it on her cheeks and nose, and then in her eyes. Her face looked sunburned and her eyes were red and swollen. "You should have told me."

"When? In the middle of the fire?"

He growled in frustration. She could be annoyingly rational. "I'm calling the doctor."

"Cade, no. Please. We learned all about pepper spray at Quantico. I know how to treat it. This looks a lot worse than it is." She gave him a little smile. "Most of the redness will be gone by morning. Besides, like I said, I don't want anyone to know about this. Misty's attack and the fire are bad enough."

"What are you hoping to accomplish by keeping it quiet?"

"Maybe whoever's doing this will think they're getting away with it. Or get mad because nobody's making a big deal about it. Either way, I'm hoping we can catch them off guard."

Made sense, in her irritatingly rational way. But other, more pressing matters held his attention. He was still rubbing her arms, but what was supposed to be a comforting touch had turned into a caress.

She looked slender and delicate in her pink pajamas. He couldn't keep his eyes off the tight peaks of her breasts hidden by a thin layer of silk. Her breasts, her slim waist, that perfect behind. Everything about her attracted him.

Not even her splotchy red face and swollen eyelids spoiled her allure. To his chagrin, his body began to react. Suddenly he was as turned on as a randy kid. Except right now, his primary feeling wasn't horniness. He felt protective and caring.

He touched her cheek, where the redness almost hid her freckles. "Does it hurt?"

She gave him a sheepish little smile. "Please do not hand me that old joke."

"What joke?" He frowned at her.

"You know—does your face hurt? Because it's killing me."

He laughed. "You think I'm that mean?"

She shrugged. "I don't know. A lot of folks in this town are."

He pushed a stray hair back from her forehead. "Not me."

He couldn't believe how many colors danced in her eyes, even surrounded by pink, swollen flesh. Hazel eyes had always seemed sort of flat and uninteresting to him. But Laurel's were green and amber, with a touch of blue and a few specks of an odd rust color. *Fascinating.*

His arousal stirred even more as he moved his gaze from her eyes to her mouth. Her lips were moist and looked infinitely kissable.

"Cade?" she whispered.

"Hmm?"

Her tongue flicked out to moisten her lips and he felt a groan start deep in his throat. Suddenly, he realized just how close he was to kissing her.

He had a crime scene—another crime scene—to deal with. He needed to focus.

Besides, she was only here for the weekend. He could rein in his inconveniently raging libido for two days.

Right now, he needed to know exactly what had happened. "When did you notice the fire?"

Laurel moistened her lips. "When I came out of the bathroom, I smelled smoke and saw the flickering light. Whoever was in here must have started it while I was outside dealing with the car alarm. They didn't have time once I came back inside."

"So they set off the car alarm, sneaked in and started the fire while you were outside, then maced you when you came in, and ran."

She nodded. "I think they were trying to find and destroy the pictures. Misty's and mine."

"Or trying to kill you."

Laurel stared at him. "Kill me? No. I just got here. No one has a reason to kill me."

"Think about it. Everything was fine until you showed up. You're stirring up things someone wants to keep buried."

"So you think I'm right about Wendell's death?"

"I don't know, but it sure looks like somebody's trying to stop you from nosing around."

"Oh! I need to check on my photos." She turned and headed toward the back of the house.

Cade followed.

In the guest bedroom, she reached for the jacket she'd tossed across a chair and felt in the pockets. With a sigh of relief she pulled the pictures out. "They're here."

"I'll put them in the evidence room."

"So you *do* think I'm right about Wendell."

He shrugged. "Whoever's behind this is desperate. They're risking lives to keep something quiet. These pictures could be the key. I'd feel better if they were locked up. Plus, it'd be nice if you weren't attacked again before daybreak."

She sent him a narrow gaze.

"Or ever, if I can help it," he amended with a small smile. He took the pictures from her and slid them into a plastic bag from his pocket.

"Okay." He looked at his watch and sighed. "Almost 4:00 a.m. I think we've had quite enough excitement for this weekend."

"And this is just Friday. I've still got the reunion to get through."

"Are you sure you want to stay? It's obvious you're a target. I've called Misty's parents. They're coming up from Florida this morning to take her home with them. You should consider going back to D.C."

"Are you kidding me? I'm not going anywhere. I believe Wendell was murdered, and I'm not leaving here until I can prove how he died."

He sighed. "Well, Special Agent Laurel Gillespie, you've certainly stirred up a hornet's nest. Get dressed. You're going to have to come with me. You sure can't stay here."

She looked around at the mess. "I guess not."

He picked up her jacket. "Here. Put this on." He held it for her but she stopped.

"Oh, my God! I dropped my gun when I got maced. I tried to find it but my eyes were burning too much."

"Where is it?"

"It should be somewhere in the foyer, but—"

"Okay. We'll look."

It didn't take two minutes to realize that the weapon was nowhere to be found.

"Whoever attacked me must have picked it up."

Cade swallowed that information. *Not good.* Not good at all. "Whoever's doing this is armed."

Chapter Four

Laurel quickly dressed and packed her small suitcase. "I let them get my weapon. What a rookie mistake," she said to Cade.

"You were blinded by Mace."

Cade's words didn't make Laurel feel any better. She shook her head. "First thing the FBI teaches you—hang on to your weapon no matter what."

"You're right. It's not good that your attacker has your gun. Do you have a backup?"

She thought about the little Smith & Wesson in her suitcase and nodded. "I've got to report my weapon missing, though." She didn't want to think about what her boss, Mitch Decker, would say. He was kind and understanding—to a point. But he expected a lot of his agents—as much as he did of himself. Laurel hated to disappoint him.

Cade touched her arm. "Come on, we've got to find you a place to sleep."

Laurel shook off his touch. "I need to go through that mess. If there's anything left, I need to find it. The only reason someone would do this is if they were afraid of what Misty's pictures might show." She headed toward the dining room. "At least he didn't have time to find what he was looking for, or he wouldn't have bothered to set the fire."

"You need to see a doctor about your eyes and then get some sleep."

She ignored him. The dining room was a charred, sodden mess. Her stomach sank to her toes. "Poor Misty. He tried to burn every photo she had."

She picked up a partially burned snapshot, then another and another.

"I'll have Shelton box them up," Cade said. "He and Fred can go through them tomorrow." He took the snapshots from her hand and laid them back on the table.

She picked them up again. "I don't want anyone to see these. I'd rather the attacker think they all burned up."

"Okay then, I'll get my dad to do it."

She looked up. "Your dad? Oh, Cade, I never asked about him. Misty told me he'd had a stroke. Is he okay?"

"He's doing fine. He has a little trouble with his speech, but there's nothing wrong with his mind or his body."

Her eyes were starting to burn again. She covered them with her palms. "I'm so glad he's okay. It was wonderful of you to come back to stay with him. With James's death and then the stroke, he must have been so glad to have you." Misty had told her at the time that Cade had just finished his training at Quantico. He'd given up his FBI job to come home and help his father.

Cade nodded. "Yeah. Come on. You need to see a doctor."

"I told you, this will be better after I get some sleep. If you want to do something for me, check Misty's medicine cabinet. See if she has some saline eyewash and a bottle of witch hazel."

He frowned. "Witch hazel?"

"Misty hasn't changed a thing in this house since her

parents moved to Florida. I'd bet money her mother kept witch hazel in her bathroom cabinet."

While Cade went to check the bathroom, Laurel closed her eyes and went over the timeline of her attack. But try her best, she couldn't put herself into the mind of the perpetrator. This time she was the victim and that was all she could think about—how helpless she'd felt against the Mace and the blanket.

The attacker had slipped into the house while she was dealing with the car alarm. He must have dumped the photos and lit the fire in record time, because she couldn't have been outside more than four or five minutes, and the fire was already raging when she came out of the bathroom.

"Here you go. You were right."

Laurel opened her eyes to a tiny slit and saw the plastic bottle of witch hazel in Cade's hand.

"Of course, who knows how old it is."

"I don't care," she said.

"Let's go. I just talked to Mr. Holder. He owns a bed-and-breakfast near my house."

"What about Harriet?"

"The cat will be fine tonight. We'll do something about her tomorrow."

"I'll drive my car."

Cade took her by the shoulders and pointed her in the direction of the front door. "No, you won't. Not with those eyes. We'll get it tomorrow."

She gave in. "Don't forget the photos."

"Not a chance." His voice held a note of irony.

LAUREL SLEPT with cotton pads soaked in witch hazel on her eyes. She only got about three hours' sleep but her eyes felt much better. She put on her makeup very carefully.

Then she paced. It was nine o'clock. Where was Cade?

She'd already talked to her boss Mitch about the loss of her weapon. He'd told her where to get the forms she needed to fill out.

Fuming, she looked around for a phone book. If Cade thought he was going to leave her sitting around nursing her eyes all day, he had another thing coming. She had too much to do. They had to question all the members of the Reunion Committee, go through Misty's photos and Wendell's case file and prepare for the party.

It was obvious she'd stirred up old secrets and fears. She felt sure that one of the people who'd overheard her phone call to Misty had attacked her. Someone with a big secret to hide.

Speaking of phone calls, she wasn't waiting another minute for Cade. She retrieved her cell phone, dialed Information and got the chief of police's cell number.

Just as she was about to press Call she heard a banging on the door.

Cade.

She threw the door open so hard it crashed against the wall. "Where have you been?" she demanded. "It's late."

His eyes flashed and his mouth turned up into the crooked grin that knocked her socks off every time. "I'm fine, thanks. How're you?"

She rolled her eyes. "Sorry. Good morning. We need to question all the members of the Reunion Committee."

Cade sidestepped her and closed the door. "I stopped and talked to Mrs. Gardner."

"Who?"

"The elderly lady across the street from Misty. She's the one who called me yesterday to report that someone was lurking. *You.* She told me people had been lurking around the street all day. So I wanted to find out what she knew."

"And—?"

"*All day* turned out to be twice."

"Twice?"

"Yeah. It fits. She saw movement around Misty's house at six and then again around eight o'clock. But she couldn't identify anyone. Apparently she doesn't see so well. Speaking of eyes—"

His hand on her arm surprised her.

"Let me look at yours."

"My eyes are fine. I told you—"

He placed his hands on either side of her head and examined her face and eyes. His warm palms cradled her cheeks protectively, and his blue gaze swept across the sensitive skin around her eyes like the ghost of a touch.

She'd already examined her face in the mirror, so she knew that although the swelling and redness were better, she looked as if she'd been on a crying jag.

"They still hurt." His words were a statement, not a question. His gaze was soft, and it drifted down toward her mouth.

Laurel swallowed hard. She was getting way too into his gentle concern. She backed up and pushed his hands away. "I'm fine. I'll wear sunglasses and tell people I have allergies."

She started to put her cell phone into her purse, then thought of something. "Give me your cell phone number."

"What? So you can call me at the crack of dawn?"

She opened her mouth to retort, but he held up his hand. "That was a joke. Here."

They exchanged numbers.

"Thanks," Laurel said as she checked her backup

weapon and stuck it in the paddle holster that rested at the small of her back. "I don't suppose you've set up interview times with the Reunion Committee?"

He propped an arm on the mantel and sent her an irritated glance. "Not yet. I figured we could go by my dad's and check out the pictures he found."

Her pulse jumped. "He found pictures already? In all that mess?"

"He gets up early."

"Why didn't you tell me?" She grabbed the doorknob and flung the door open, then looked back at him, catching him staring at her bottom. He hadn't moved from his slouch against the mantel.

"Well? Are you coming?"

He muttered something under his breath. She thought it was *not a chance*.

CADE FOLLOWED Laurel out to his pickup. She was determined—he had to give her that. Her eyes were still swollen and bloodshot, but she hadn't complained at all. All her concentration and energy were aimed at finding out who had attacked her friend and her.

He opened the passenger-side door and stood back to let her climb in. Her skirt was knee-length and slim, and it rode up her thigh as she stepped up onto the running board of the pickup and into the cab. She glanced at him quickly, then smoothed her skirt, tugging on the hem.

He shut the door, a smile playing around his lips. Another fact about her—she dressed in what women used to call the *power suit*. He supposed it helped her feel and look more businesslike and competent, but she couldn't bring herself to completely hide her femininity. If she really wanted to play up her competence and play down her looks and sexuality, that skirt could be a lot looser and longer, and her shoes could have lower heels.

He went around and climbed into the truck and took off. It only took about three minutes to get to his dad's house. Cade didn't look forward to introducing Laurel to him. He couldn't be sure what Dad would talk about. He might tell her about Cade's experience with the FBI, or he might go off on a long discussion about James.

Cade was also a little afraid that she might have trouble understanding his father, and he did not want his dad embarrassed if she got impatient.

However, he needn't have worried. She charmed his father, and seemed to be charmed by him. They bent over the photos together, leaving Cade craning his neck to see. He finally gave up and went into the kitchen and made coffee.

Then he called to set up interviews with Kathy Adler, Debra Evans, Mary Sue Nelson and Ralph Langston, sipping his coffee as he listened to their tirades about how busy they were.

When he brought coffee to his dad and Laurel, they were laughing about something. Cade felt a twinge of jealousy. He hadn't seen his dad laugh since his stroke. More accurately, since James died.

Laurel grabbed the coffee cup as if it were a lifeline. She wrapped both hands around it and took a long swallow. It seemed to transform her.

"Ah, that's good." She smiled at him. "Unfortunately, I'm addicted."

Cade nodded. "We'd better get going. We've got our first interview in—" he checked his watch "—ten minutes."

"Really? Great!"

Cade took the box of photos from his dad and stuck it

under his arm. "I'll run these by the station and lock them in the evidence room on our way."

"Good. Now I won't have to worry about them any more." She took another hefty swallow of coffee. "Mr. Dupree, I have to know what kind of coffee this is."

To his surprise, his dad took her by the hand and led her into the kitchen. "It's a blend. I mix a pound of medium-roast Arabica with a quarter pound of Jamaican Blue Mountain. Then I put in a few tablespoon of hazelnut flavor blend."

"Wonderful. I'll try that. The touch of hazelnut is inspired." After reluctantly setting the cup down, she turned and held out her hand to his dad. "Thank you so much. We couldn't have done it without you."

"Glad to help. The bigges' mystery I solve these days is where my golf ball rolls. Come back to see me."

Laurel leaned over and kissed his dad on the cheek. "I will, and I'll be on the lookout for dark chocolate-covered cherries."

His dad's eyes lit up. "Tha'd be great."

As she passed Cade going out the front door, he murmured, "Dark chocolate cherries?"

She sent him a smile over her shoulder. "His favorite. But you know that."

A twinge of sadness hit his chest. He rubbed it. "*His* favorite? I thought he bought them for—" He bit off the rest of the sentence. *For James.* Just like everything else.

Laurel did a double take. "Sorry, what did you say?"

"Nothing." He opened the front door for her. "Dad, bye," he called. "I'll see you later."

As he followed her to his truck, he pushed aside thoughts of his brother. Concentrating on Laurel's well-rounded backside helped.

"So what's *your* favorite?"

"Huh?" He almost plowed into her. In a finessing move worthy of a gold-medal ice skater, he managed to avoid a collision while at the same time sliding around to open the passenger-side door of the pickup.

"What's your favorite candy?"

Great. Now his brain was back where he didn't want it to be. He had a vision of his dad coming home with a box of dark chocolate cherries and James grabbing for them. He didn't bother to answer her.

When they were in the truck, Laurel tapped the box Cade had set on the console between them. "Your dad did a great job. He found a couple of shots that Misty's dad took that were a wider-angle than mine. You need to look at them. A lot of them were burned too badly, but there are a couple that the FBI lab should be able to analyze. Not only can you see the ring in the photo, but there's a portion of a face. I can't tell who it is. I'm hoping the lab guys can enhance it enough to recognize."

"FBI lab?" Cade took a corner more aggressively than he needed to. "So did someone put you in charge?"

"I was going to ask you again about requesting the FBI's help."

Irritation crowded up into his chest, squeezing it. "With what?" he snapped. "A flimsy theory about a ten-year-old picture?"

"Setting aside for the moment that the Unsolved Mysteries Division is in the *business* of reinvestigating old cases, we also have two assaults in the same night, plus a fire intended to burn the pictures that support my flimsy theory. So you might want to pay attention to it."

Her voice was cold, but he heard an undercurrent of something he couldn't identify. "And you might want to stop right there. I don't have to let you sit in on these interviews."

"No, you don't. And I don't have to wait for your request. If I present my *flimsy evidence* to my boss, he'll get me assigned through the governor if necessary."

"I didn't say your evidence was flimsy."

"Oh, right. Big difference. Flimsy theory—flimsy evidence."

He kept his mouth shut as he turned onto the road to the creek bank.

"I remember this. Too bad this road wasn't paved when we were in high school."

Cade glanced over at her. The road below the old high school had always been a popular parking spot. "Spend a lot of time parked down there?"

Her cheeks turned pink. "No. But I'm sure you did."

He'd been down there a few times, but he'd always felt that making out with a girl while other kids were doing the same a few feet away was a little sleazy. "You'd be surprised," he muttered as he pulled up in front of the Visitor Center.

Laurel stared at the building. "This is Ralph's Visitor Center?"

Cade gestured. "See where they're breaking ground? By the time they're done, the Swinging Oak and the swimming hole will be history. Hell, knowing Ralph Langston, he's liable to put a fountain in the bend of the creek." He sighed. "Still, the convention complex should be good for Dusty Springs."

"You almost sound like you believe that."

A scowl marred his handsome features. "Let's go. We're late for our first interview."

"Why are we questioning them here?" Laurel asked, as she climbed out of the truck.

"The party's tonight. They're going to be working here all day."

"Oh, and heaven forbid the CeeGees or Ralph, the moneybags, be inconvenienced. Fine. Who's first?"

"Kathy. She's got a hair appointment this afternoon."

"Wow. She really *is* working hard," she drawled. "Wouldn't want to let a police investigation interfere with her day."

Cade stopped her at the door. "Look. I get how you feel about these women. Am I going to be able to count on you to be professional? If not, I can't have you in the room."

"Sorry." She felt her face burn. She didn't like being reprimanded by him. "I would never say anything in front of a witness or a suspect. I was just venting."

He opened the door.

Laurel stopped him with a hand on his arm. "Cade, can we keep Wendell's death out of it until we've had a chance to look at the photos?"

He looked through the glass door as if he were thinking about it. "No problem," he finally said.

When they entered, Kathy was pacing in front of a small conference room with an unlit cigarette in her hand.

"It's about time, Cade. I told you I could spare you ten minutes." She looked at her watch. "Half of that's already gone."

She started to put the cigarette in her mouth, then looked at it and muttered a curse. "I'm so tired of these no-smoking buildings," she complained as she dug in her purse and came up with a cough drop.

Laurel noticed Kathy's hand shaking. She watched her closely as Cade apologized for being late and held the door for her. She looked better than she had the night before—barely. Her makeup was smeared and her eyes were puffy. She'd been drinking already.

Kathy laid down her unlit cigarette as Cade explained why he was questioning her.

"I didn't see anything. I didn't hear anything," Kathy said, crumpling the cellophane wrapper.

"Hang on just a minute, Kathy." Cade reached in his pocket for a miniature tape recorder and set it on the table. "Do you object to being taped?"

"Would it matter if I did?"

"Kathy, I need your cooperation." Cade leaned forward. "You're a leader in this town. If people see you doing the right thing, they will, too."

Kathy actually preened at Cade's words. "Well, I trust you. You won't ask anything that might embarrass a lady, will you?"

Cade's mouth widened into that killer grin as he pushed the record button and recited the necessary identification and date and time stamp information.

"Have you been inside Misty's house?"

"Well, of course. I was at the Reunion Committee meeting on Monday. Are you trying to trick me, Cade Dupree?"

He shook his head. "You walked up the street to check on Misty when the EMTs arrived, didn't you? What did you do after that?"

"You know what I did. That officer of yours walked me home. I read for a while and then went to sleep."

"So you didn't hear the car alarm go off later? Your house is only three doors down from Misty's."

Kathy shrugged. "What can I tell you? I'm a sound sleeper."

I'll bet, Laurel thought.

Cade leaned back in his chair. "What about Harrison? Did the car alarm wake him up?"

Kathy's mouth thinned and lines appeared around her lips and nose and forehead. "I have no idea."

"You don't know if your husband woke up when the alarm went off?"

"Not that it's any of your business, Cade Dupree, but no. Harrison was in his study, passed out from brandy as usual."

She straightened her shoulders, glanced at Laurel for the first time, then stood. "I have to leave now. Please try not to take up too much of everyone's time. We're trying to put out all the last-minute fires before the big party tonight."

"One more question. Where were you around six o'clock yesterday evening?"

"Six o'clock?" For a split second Kathy looked blank, then she blinked. "Was that when Misty was attacked?"

"Do you remember where you were?"

She looked at the filter tip of her cigarette. Her fingers trembled. "I was at home." She took a deep breath. "Taking a nap."

"Alone, I take it."

She blinked slowly and touched her finger to the corner of her lip, as if smoothing her lipstick. "Of course."

"Thanks, Kathy. Send in Ralph."

Kathy eyed Cade. "Well, aren't we all *Law & Order?*" She turned.

"Kathy," Laurel said, pulling a business card out of her purse. "There's my cell phone number. Let me know if you think of anything that might help us."

Kathy took the card between two fingers as if it were tainted. She stuck it in her purse without looking at it or at Laurel, then she swept out the door.

"She's been drinking," Laurel whispered to Cade.

He arched a brow at her. "You just figured that out?"

"No. I *figured* it out last night." Laurel wanted to stick

out her tongue at him or give him some other rude adolescent gesture but she restrained herself. "But drinking in the morning? She's a mess."

A wrinkle appeared between Cade's brows. "Sometimes I wonder if she's as big a mess as she likes to appear. I have a feeling it suits her to be underestimated."

"Well, she's obviously an alcoholic."

"What do you think about her alibi for yesterday evening? Taking a nap—alone?"

"I don't believe it. You know her. She's hardly charitable about her husband. Could she be having an affair?"

Cade shook his head. "More likely she was passed out."

The door opened and Ralph Langston blustered in.

Laurel was surprised. Skinny, nerdy Ralph from high school had changed—a lot. Here was one classmate she would not have recognized. She studied him as he shook Cade's hand and then hers. He'd had some kind of plastic surgery. His jaw looked more square. He had more hair than he'd had in school, too, and the pullover shirt and khaki pants he wore revealed muscular arms and abs and thighs. He must have gained sixty pounds since she'd last seen him—and it looked like it was all muscle.

He sat at the head of the table and glared at Cade and her like a boss about to reprimand his employees.

"So, Cade. What can I do for you?"

"When did you get into town?"

Ralph sat back in his chair and smiled. "Come on, Cade. I've been in and out of town for weeks, supervising the building of my convention center. Just cut to the chase. Where was I last night? I'd be happy to tell you, if I'm being charged with anything. Otherwise, I'll keep my mouth shut. To do otherwise would compromise a nice woman."

"You're saying you were with a woman last night? For how long? Give me the specifics."

Ralph certainly had the young executive act down. He had the suit, the body and the hair weave. But he was creeping her out. He was too smooth, too coy.

"We met at eight, had dinner, and then—" He glanced at Laurel. "Let's just say I left after midnight."

"You were at her house?"

Ralph waved a hand. "Again, no comment."

"Will your lady friend verify that you were there?"

Ralph shook his head. "No. Absolutely not."

"Tell me about the meeting at Misty's house."

"The meeting? You mean Monday? What about it? Misty's house was dark and musty, but the meeting was productive."

"Do you recall Misty getting a phone call while you were there?" Cade asked.

Ralph's gaze flickered to Laurel. "I went to the bathroom and when I came back into the dining room Misty was talking on the phone. I didn't pay much attention to the conversation."

"So you don't know who she was talking to?"

"Sure." He smiled at Laurel. "She told us all after she hung up."

"What else did she tell you?"

"Nothing. Just that Laurel was going to stay with her this weekend."

Cade stood and walked behind Ralph. "Okay. If you can't give me something to prove to me that you weren't anywhere near Misty's house last night, I'll have to ask to search your hotel room."

Ralph obviously didn't like Cade standing behind him. He smoothed the back of his hair nervously and struggled not to turn around.

"Give me a break. First of all, you won't find anything. Second, no judge would give you a warrant based solely on my refusal to embarrass someone just to give myself an alibi."

"All right," Cade said, still behind him. "If I won't find anything, it can't hurt to let me look."

Irritation and something else flashed in Ralph's eyes. He spread his hands. "You're asking me to prove a negative. I'm thinking it's *your* job to find proof. Now if you'll excuse me—"

Cade stepped out of the way as Ralph pushed his chair back.

"I have a party to finalize, and thanks to you and your questioning, we'll be lucky if we're ready by the time the party starts."

Cade put his hand on the door. "One last thing. Where were you at around six o'clock yesterday evening?"

"Around six? I was in my hotel room, getting ready for my date."

"Can anyone corroborate that?"

"I called Kathy about that time—a question about the decorations."

Laurel sat up straight. "Kathy said she was taking a nap."

Ralph pulled his cell phone out of his pocket and punched a couple of buttons. "I called her at 6:11 p.m. on the dot and talked to her for two minutes and seventeen seconds. Are you saying she doesn't remember talking to me?" Ralph shook his head and locked gazes with Cade. "Poor girl. She really needs help." He reached for the doorknob.

"Ralph." Laurel stood. "Did you call Kathy's home phone?"

Ralph looked thoughtful. "No. Her cell."

She exchanged a glance with Cade. Kathy could have been anywhere, even inside Misty's house.

Ralph turned as he stepped through the door. "Laurel, you look nice. Nice."

Shuddering inwardly, Laurel handed him her card. "Call me if you think of anything else."

Ralph pointed a finger at her and winked, then closed the door behind him.

"He is so creepy," she commented.

Cade flashed her a quick grin. "Creepy, maybe. Cagey, definitely. I'd bet you a hundred dollars he talked to his lawyer last night or this morning."

She shook her head. "I'm not taking that bet. Do you think he's the one who attacked Misty and me?"

"You need to answer that question. Was it a man who maced you and threw you down?"

She closed her eyes and replayed the attack in her head. "I don't know. I didn't see anything—the perp must have been wearing black. And he barely touched me. Just maced me and tossed the blanket over my head when I came inside. I hit the floor like a rock."

"Footsteps? Aftershave or perfume? Anything?"

"I'm sorry. I don't remember smelling anything. I didn't even smell the smoke until later."

"And you said you were outside about five minutes?"

"At the most. Not long enough for anyone to search for the photos."

"What about after you were maced?"

"I suppose by the time I crawled into the bathroom and washed my eyes out, it could have been five more minutes. I don't know. The fire got so big so quickly."

"Right. Kit said something about dried-out wood and rotten draperies."

A tentative knock sounded on the door, and Debra peeked in. "Should I come in now, or did you want me to wait?"

Cade stood. "No. Come in. We're ready."

Debra chose a seat a couple of chairs down from Laurel. She clasped her hands in her lap. Her gaze flitted between the two of them like a frightened bird. "I don't know what I can tell you. I don't know any more than I did last night."

"What did you do after Misty was taken to the hospital?"

"I went home."

"So you didn't hear the fire trucks later?"

She shook her head. "I went to bed early."

"What about earlier? What were you doing at around six o'clock?"

"Six o'clock?" Debra's eyes grew wide. "I was at the grocery store. Then I went over to Daddy's and cooked supper for him."

"Did you see anyone you knew?"

"Now that I think about it, no. How funny."

"When did you leave your dad's?"

"I think it was nearly seven. When I got home my husband complained about his supper being late."

"So you don't know who attacked Misty."

Debra caught her lower lip between her teeth and lowered her gaze to her pink fingertips. "No."

Debra did know something. Laurel was sure of it. She'd be easy to crack, too. Laurel opened her mouth to press her for information but Cade stopped her with a subtle gesture.

"But you have an idea, don't you?" he said gently.

Debra looked up and Laurel saw tears glistening in her eyes. "No! No. Why would you say that, Cade? I don't know anything. I promise."

Cade leaned back in his chair and studied Debra. Laurel studied him. He exuded strength and protectiveness, and Debra was obviously drawn to that like a moth to a flame.

Laurel felt the other woman's tug of war. Debra couldn't reveal what she knew, but she wanted to please Cade.

It occurred to Laurel that Debra had always been a follower, always been a people pleaser. She'd been let into Kathy's elite circle because she'd fawned over her. Laurel remembered something else, too. She'd never seen Debra be mean to anyone. She'd followed Kathy's instructions, but she was always apologetic. Could she have picked the lock on Misty's front door and sneaked in and hit her? Laurel doubted it. She knew for a fact that it wasn't Debra who'd attacked *her*.

"Cade, please." Debra fidgeted. "Stop staring at me. I can't tell you anything."

He nodded. "Okay. You can go. Here." He held out a hand to Laurel. "Take one of Agent Gillespie's cards in case you remember something."

Biting her tongue, Laurel handed him a card. He gave it to Debra.

As soon as the door closed behind Debra, Laurel spoke. "What are you doing? You almost had her. Ten more seconds and she'd have spilled everything she knew."

He shook his head. "She was about to break. I had to back off. I didn't want her to start crying or *all* the questioning would be over."

"Maybe." Laurel wasn't totally convinced. Was Cade a big softie who couldn't resist tears? Or was he just very smart?

Chapter Five

"Debra knows something," Laurel insisted to Cade. "I'm sure of it. We need to talk to her again."

"My guess is she knows a lot, but she's too afraid of somebody to talk."

"Kathy."

He nodded and stood. "I'll get Mary Sue."

Just then the door burst open. Kathy breezed in, bringing with her the smell of cigarette smoke. "Are you finished yet?" she demanded. "We need this room to store supplies in."

Cade took her elbow and guided her out of the room. "Mary Sue and Ann Noble are the last ones. Just a few more minutes and we'll be out of your hair."

When Mary Sue came in, she paid about as much attention to Laurel as she did to the floor—none. Her whole attention was aimed at Cade.

Still amused by Mary Sue's blatant flirting at the hospital, Laurel tried to catch Cade's eye. He ignored her.

"Mary Sue, you remember me from high school, don't you?" she said, sliding a card across the table toward her.

Mary Sue's eyes barely flickered toward her. She picked up the card and glanced at it. "Vaguely," she said, and smiled at Cade.

"Mary Sue. Look at me." She resisted the urge to snap her fingers in front of the woman's face. "Do you know anything about the break-in at Misty's house? Or the fire later that night?"

"Of course not." She shot Laurel an annoyed glance, then looked back at Cade. To Laurel's surprise, she actually batted her eyelashes.

He cleared his throat and sat back in his chair. "Where were you around six o'clock last night?"

"Oh, heavens, Cade," she said, waving a perfectly manicured hand. "I don't know. Yesterday was a very busy day. I was probably picking up my boys at soccer practice."

"Probably?" Laurel repeated.

"After that I was at home with my husband and children. Someone called me about Misty, so I called my friend Dolly at the florist shop, got her to whip me up a bouquet and took it to the hospital. You were there."

"Who called you?"

She swished a manicured hand through the air. "I don't remember. I was so distraught about Misty. One of my neighbors, I suppose." She glanced at Cade coyly.

Laurel grimaced internally at Mary Sue's posturing. Did she actually think that southern-belle routine worked?

She glanced at Cade and caught a look of utter misery on his face. She had to bite her lip to keep from laughing. He looked like a man facing the gallows.

"What about the time of the fire?"

Mary Sue shrugged. "In the middle of the night? I was asleep. I didn't hear about the fire until this morning." She gave Laurel all her attention for the first time. "Was that you that nearly got burned up?"

Laurel literally bit her tongue to keep from lashing out at the prim and vacuous woman. "On Monday," she said through gritted teeth, "you were at a meeting at Misty's house."

"Was that just Monday? It seems like a week ago."

Today's Saturday. It *was* a week ago. "You were there when Misty answered the phone. You heard her call me by name, right?"

Mary Sue looked blank. "I remember a phone call. Misty mentioned pictures. I thought it must be the drug store, calling her about a roll of film."

"You didn't hear her mention Wendell Vance or graduation night?" Laurel asked. Mary Sue set her teeth on edge. She couldn't possibly be that out of tune with the world, could she?

"No. At least, I don't think so."

"All right, Mary Sue. You can go. Please ask Ann Noble to come in." Cade's tone was commanding, so Laurel kept her mouth shut while Mary Sue managed to touch his arm twice before he ushered her out the door.

Laurel put her head between her hands. "Oh, my gosh. Is she always like that?"

"Far as I know. What was she like in high school?"

"I have no idea. I never talked to the CeeGees. I wasn't worth their time."

"That bothers you?"

She laughed. "Not anymore. I think we can eliminate Mary Sue from the suspect list. She couldn't possibly have planned or carried out the attack on Misty."

The door opened and Ann Noble stepped in. Her navy blazer and plaid skirt were impeccably pressed, and the low-heeled navy shoes she wore were polished to a high shine. Her glasses hung by a practical cord around her neck, and she clutched a leather folder. Her only concession to fashion was her perfectly applied makeup.

"Chief Dupree." She nodded at Cade and then held her hand out to Laurel. "Hello. I'm Ann Noble, personal assistant to the mayor. I don't believe we've met."

"No, we haven't." Laurel stood and took Ann Noble's hand. "I'm Special Agent Laurel Gillespie, with the FBI. Please sit down."

"Do you have a card, Agent Gillespie?"

Proactive. Laurel handed her a business card.

"Ms. Noble, thank you for coming down here." Cade used his killer smile to full advantage. "We just have a couple of questions. Were you at the Reunion Committee meeting at Misty Waller's house on Monday?"

"Yes, of course." She perched her glasses on her nose, opened her folder and took out a sheet of paper. "I'm sure you'd like to track my movements since then. So I took the liberty of preparing a record of my appointments and locations since the meeting at Ms. Waller's house. I'll give you a few minutes to look that over and you can let me know if you have any questions." She extracted a second sheet of paper and handed it to Laurel.

Cade sent Laurel a furtive glance. She had to bite her lip to hide her amusement as she skimmed the sheet. Ann Noble was wasted in Dusty Springs. She should work for the State Department. She might actually accomplish herding cats.

"You're not originally from here, are you?" Cade asked her.

Ms. Noble let her glasses drop to her chest. "No. I moved here six years ago from Southhaven. I'd known the mayor in law school."

"You're a lawyer?" Laurel asked.

She shook her head. "Regretfully I had to leave school when my mother became ill."

"How did you end up on the Reunion Committee?"

"The Mayor wanted to be sure the committee had everything they needed for a successful reunion. It's part of his community involvement campaign."

"Tell us about the meeting at Misty Waller's house."

"Of course. Although as I just pointed out, the only reason I'm on the committee at all is as a representative of the mayor. I have no personal connection to any of the members. I'm happy to help, though. I do have very good powers of observation."

"That's good to hear."

Ms. Noble went through an exhaustive play-by-play of the entire meeting. "So we were just about to wrap things up when the phone rang."

Cade's body language shifted slightly. He was intent on what Ann Noble was going to say.

"Misty said, 'Hi, Laurel.' After she listened for a moment, she said, 'Photographs from graduation night? I don't remember.' She said she'd look to see if she had any with Wendell in them as soon as the meeting was over."

Laurel gaped. Powers of observation, hah. Ann Noble had an eidetic memory. She'd quoted practically word for word what was said.

Cade's gaze flickered her way then back to Ann Noble, who directed her next comment to Laurel.

"The fact that Misty mentioned photographs and the name Wendell apparently upset you, Special Agent Gillespie. I can only speculate, but I assume you didn't want her talking in front of the others, since you ended the call almost immediately."

"What about the other people in the room?" Cade asked. "Did any of them react to what Misty said?"

Ann frowned. "I did notice that Kathy Adler seemed extremely interested in the phone call. None of the others reacted. Not really."

Not really? From the look on Cade's face, he was thinking the same thing she was. Ann Noble wasn't one to prevaricate. "You noticed something else, didn't you?" Laurel asked.

"I hesitate to say anything, because it's just an impression—" She paused for an instant. "But when Misty mentioned the name Wendell, Mary Sue Nelson gasped, and Debra Honeycutt grew white as a sheet."

"What about Langston? How did he react?" Cade asked.

Ann picked up her glasses and inspected them. She flicked a speck of lint off one lens with the tip of a nail. "He seemed more bored than anything. I don't think sitting in a roomful of women drinking iced tea is his thing."

"So he was in the room the whole time?"

Ann held her glasses up to the light.

Stalling for time.

"As I recall, he may have excused himself just prior to the call. But he returned quickly."

Cade leaned forward. "What were you doing last evening from—let's say—six o'clock on."

Her neck flushed. "I had a date."

"Starting at six o'clock?"

"I got in from work, bathed and changed and my date arrived around eight."

Eight o'clock. The same time as Ralph's date. Laurel glanced at Cade, but he was studying Ann.

"Where did you and your date go?"

Ann's flush traveled up to her cheeks. "We—stayed in."

"Who was your date?" Laurel asked her.

Ann sat upright and sent Laurel a quelling look. "Is that pertinent?"

Cade spoke up. "Unless we know who you were with, you leave yourself with no alibi."

"*Alibi?* Surely you're not serious."

"Oh, yes, ma'am, I'm very serious. What time was your date over?"

Ann pursed her lips. "Very late."

"So you won't offer any proof of where you were for the whole night?"

She glanced at her watch. "I really should be getting back to my office. I'm supposed to coordinate a teleconference for the mayor in about twenty minutes." She slid her chair back and picked up the leather folder.

Cade stood as she did. "On a Saturday?"

"Of course." Her mouth twisted in a smug smile. "I am available to the mayor any time he needs me."

"If you decide to come clean about your date, please call me."

"Certainly." She twisted the doorknob and jerked the door open. On the verge of bolting, she froze, then closed the door again and turned around.

"If I disclose who I was with last night, can I count on your discretion?" A bright flush rose from her neck to redden her face.

Laurel spoke up. "We'll do everything we can to keep you out of it, depending on what you're about to tell us."

Ann Noble took a long breath. "I was with George Honeycutt."

"Debra's husband?"

"Yes. I trust this won't have to come out?"

"As Laurel said, we'll do our best."

The woman felt behind her for the doorknob and escaped from the room.

Cade stood, closed the door and turned around. "That was interesting."

"Do you think Debra knows?"

He shook his head. "Something didn't ring true about Ann's last-second decision to tell us."

"I know. There's something else going on there."

Their eyes met. "Think she was lying about Honeycutt?"

"I have no idea. Still, her affair with Honeycutt doesn't explain why she was so careful to lure us into asking what she noticed at the meeting, rather than just coming out and telling us."

"Maybe Honeycutt is a diversion. Maybe our Miss Noble isn't as noble as she looks. What if she told us that to divert our attention from the real attacker, who also had a date last night."

"Ralph Langston."

"I SO DON'T WANT to go to this thing." Laurel looked out the passenger window as Cade drove back to the bed-and-breakfast.

"The reunion party? At the most it'll be three hours. What's the big deal?"

She rolled her eyes. "Obviously you were never an over-sensitive high school girl with underdeveloped social skills."

"I can't disagree with you there. But come on. Was it really that bad?" Cade's tone was teasing.

"Not for you." Laurel remembered her junior year when Cade was a senior and the school star. He'd never once noticed her. "You were on the football team. You had tons of girlfriends."

His jaw twitched and his fingers visibly tightened on the steering wheel. "You've got me confused with my brother James."

Laurel frowned at him but his eyes were on the road. She remembered every move Cade made back in high school. She could probably list every game he played in. "You played football."

"Second team until James graduated."

"Come on, Cade. Your senior year you were everything. You have no idea how it felt to be invisible."

He didn't comment.

Once they got to Laurel's room, she took out the key to unlock the door.

"Hold it," Cade said, catching her arm. "Let me check this out."

"Check wha—?"

He stopped her with a gesture, glanced around, then drew his weapon. His movements were as quiet and graceful as a big cat. As he approached the door with caution, she saw what he saw.

The old wooden door was closed but not locked. There was a gap between the door and the facing, and light streamed unencumbered through the narrow space where the dead bolt should have shown.

"Maybe I didn't lock—"

Cade silenced her with a look. His heart pounded as he thought back. He'd been standing right beside her when she'd locked the door. She hadn't forgotten.

He pressed his back against the wall and reached for the old brass knob with his left hand. He held his Sig Sauer in his right.

In his peripheral vision he saw Laurel draw her weapon—the backup she'd brought with her. He met her gaze and she sent him a slight nod. She was ready.

He turned the knob and pushed the door open, and then led with his gun as he entered the room. Sunlight poured in through the open curtains like a spotlight illuminating the mess spread before them.

Laurel uttered a little cry as she kicked the door closed behind her. "Oh, no! All my stuff!"

Cade stepped over a pile of filmy, lacy things that had been scattered all over the floor—*her* filmy, lacy things.

Don't go there, he ordered himself. But his brain presented him with an image of Laurel dressed in something soft and scant and sexy. He gave himself a mental shake. "You've already unpacked," he said tightly.

"Right. Everything was in the dresser or the closet."

Her voice was steadier now. She was Special Agent Gillespie. She glanced back at the door and he knew what she was thinking.

"No sign of forced entry," he said.

"Right. So if I'm the perp I have a key or—" She stopped and shook her head. "*He* has a key or knows where to get one." She put her fingers over her mouth and blew out a breath.

"What's the matter?"

"I can't do my usual thing. I can't get into the perp's head. Not when—I've never been the victim before."

"Don't try. Let's just talk it through. So the perp knows you're here. Everybody in town does by now. He lets himself in and trashes the place. Why?"

Laurel stepped over the piles of clothes and stood in front of the dresser. Her expression told Cade how spooked she was about her things being pawed over, but her stiff shoulders and tense jaw told him she was not going to let it interfere with her professional assessment of the scene.

"He's still worried about those photos. There's got to be an incriminating shot in one of them. Plus he doesn't have much time, so he dumps everything." She stepped over to the closet.

"He's getting angry and nervous," Cade added. "Why so desperate to find the photos?"

Laurel angled her head. "Because one of those shots shows his—*her*—hand on Wendell's shoulder. And if we can identify her, we'll know she's the one who attacked Misty."

Cade shook his head. "That's a conundrum. If she hadn't broken into Misty's house in the first place, she wouldn't have stirred up all this trouble and we might not be working so hard to identify her."

"It's got to be someone at that meeting. Someone who's terrified that I'll find a photo that shows her face. She knows from the phone call that I suspect Wendell's death wasn't suicide." Laurel bent down. "Look at this. Do you have an evidence bag?"

He reached into his jacket pocket. "Always," he said. "Although here in Dusty Springs there's not that much need for them."

She didn't even look up, just held out her hand. Then she opened the bag and retrieved something from the floor.

"What is it?"

She gave him an ironic look and held out the bag. "A false fingernail."

He looked at her short, unpainted nails. "You don't—"

"And neither does Ann Noble, but the CeeGees do. It had to be one of them that broke in."

"Did you notice their fingernails?"

"Didn't you?" Her lips curved upward. "Kathy, Mary Sue and Debra all had French tips, similar to this one."

"Not bad."

"Hey, I'm a woman *and* a criminologist. Unbeatable combination."

All that and sexy, too. "So did you notice Ralph's?"

"Buffed." Her mouth curled into a moue of distaste.

"And that's not all his real hair, either. He had less than that in high school."

Cade took the bag and studied the false nail for a few seconds. "Could somebody have dropped it on purpose, to create a false lead?"

"It's got glue on the back and there's a nasty scrape on the tip. Looks like it was knocked off. What I'd like to know is whether any bits of the nail stuck to it."

"DNA? You know that's not likely. We'd have to get samples from every female we suspect, not to mention whoever cleans in here."

"Let's get a warrant for DNA, just in case. I *know* this is flimsy evidence, but—"

"I guess we can try." He sealed the evidence bag. "It hasn't picked up any dust," he said as he wrote the date, time and place found and preliminary conclusions on the front.

"No. It probably hasn't been here more than a day."

"I'll get Phillips over here to dust for prints and search the room for anything else that might have been left behind. He can get a statement from Mr. Holder. So—you think this belongs to either Kathy or Debra or Mary Sue. And whichever one it is, she also attacked Misty and you and set the fire."

"Not necessarily."

Cade listened to Phillips' phone ring. "Why not necessarily? You think the nail was planted?"

"Or all three could be in cahoots." She planted a fist on her hip. "Don't give me that look. It makes sense—*if* they killed Wendell."

Three high school girls cold-bloodedly murdered Wendell Vance? And not just any girls, either—these were the most popular girls in their class, not to mention the least likely to get their hands dirty.

And they did it alone? Cade knew all three of them

slightly. They'd lived in Dusty Springs all their lives. He'd never seen one of the three doing anything more strenuous than using the elliptical trainer at the gym.

Except for the occasions when Kathy looked ragged around the edges, he'd never seen them with a hair out of place. "So which one did this? We just left them at the Visitor's Center."

Shelton answered his phone.

"Hey, Shelton," Cade said. "Bring a kit to the Holder Inn. Room Five. Dust for prints and check for trace."

"Be right there, Chief. What's up?"

"Someone broke into Special Agent Gillespie's room. Don't say anything about it just yet. Thanks, Shel." He hung up.

"How long did it take us to get here—maybe five minutes?" Laurel asked. "Anyone could have run over here from the Visitor Center, trashed the room and gotten back without us missing them."

"Somebody should have noticed. Who else was there today? The security guard." He answered his own question. "I'll talk to him. See if he saw someone leave and come back. Shelton should be here any minute. I'll get Fred to take prints from the CeeGees."

"You're going to tell Fred we suspect his daughter?"

"I don't think there's any need to worry him with that information. I'll tell him they're elimination prints. Get your stuff packed. You're going with me."

"I can't move anything. It'll compromise the crime scene."

"This is Dusty Springs, not Washington D.C. There's not much to compromise. That false nail is the best piece of evidence we're going to get."

He bent over and picked up a handful of her clothes from the floor. Unfortunately, when he straightened, he discovered that the handful he'd grabbed was filmy, lacy underwear. His fingers twitched and he swallowed hard, trying his best to stop his brain from making the leap from silky panties to silky body. Suddenly everything reminded him of sex. At least everything about *her.*

He tossed the things onto the bed. To his embarrassment, a tiny scrap of black lace clung to his fingers. He shook it off like a bug.

A muffled sound came from behind him. He shot a glare in Laurel's direction. Was she laughing at him? "Let's get going," he said gruffly. "We've got a lot to do before we have to get ready for the party."

"We?"

"Yeah. I'm your date. Did I forget to mention that?"

Her eyes widened and her cheeks turned pink. "My date?"

"You already have one?"

"No." She eyed him warily. "I guess it makes sense. You want to check out all the guests. I'm the perfect cover. Sure." She started to pick up her clothes off the floor.

Cade propped a shoulder against the wall and crossed his arms. He didn't trust himself to touch any more of her dainty little *things.* He hadn't had a whole lot of experience with girly things. He'd grown up in an all-male household after his mom died when he was eleven. And most of his relationships had been casual. He had never brought girls home with him and only rarely did he ever sleep over with them.

He realized he was watching Laurel's every move, and her every move was graceful and compact.

She glided back and forth, picking up clothes and tossing them into a suitcase. About half of her clothes were off the floor when she suddenly plopped down on the bed and pressed both hands against her mouth.

"Laurel?"

She didn't answer.

"Hey—what's the matter?" He pushed away from the wall and started toward her but she held up her hands, palms out.

"Nothing. Nothing. I'm fine." She stood and patted her cheeks. "It just occurred to me that somebody pawed through my things." She met his gaze, her face troubled. "I've never—it feels so—"

He took a step toward her and touched her shoulder. "It's okay. I'm going to make sure you're safe."

"Thank you, but that's not the problem, or at least not all of it." She swept an arm out. "It's my clothes. Whoever did this touched everything."

Oh, boy. He wasn't quite sure he understood exactly what the problem was, but he had a sinking feeling the solution was going to involve shopping. He thought fast.

"I tell you what. I've got a washer and dryer at my house. You can wash everything."

She looked at him and his heart literally melted and oozed down to his toes. That look was better than a kiss. Okay, maybe not better than a kiss, but it was a really great look. It did wonders for his self-esteem. He felt like a superhero. Just because he had a washing machine.

"Oh, Cade. Thank you. Can we go now?"

He swallowed and forced himself to look at something other than her beautiful multicolored eyes. He looked at her suitcase.

Her suitcase. A safe inanimate object to look at. "Sure. I'll get your bag." He had to give her credit. She'd packed everything into one suitcase. "You want to close it?" Once she had it closed, he picked it up and headed for the door.

"By the way, where will I be going?"

"To my house."

"I mean after I wash clothes. Where will I be staying?"

"Nobody's going to break into my house. I can be sure you're safe there."

Laurel's cheeks turned bright pink again. "Then where will you be?"

He opened the door and held it for her to precede him out. As she passed, he bent his head and whispered to her.

"Until I find out who's behind all this, I'm going to be glued to your side."

Chapter Six

"I can't wear this. You really don't have an iron?" Laurel held up the black dress that had cost her half a month's salary and looked at her reflection in the only mirror in Cade's house, the one over the dresser. There was a tiny medicine cabinet in the bathroom but it hardly qualified as a mirror.

The one-bedroom cottage barely held *him,* much less the both of them. Laurel had agreed to his outlandish plan only because she couldn't come up with a better idea.

Hah. Who was she kidding? She was here because he hadn't given her a choice.

"Surely there's somewhere else you can *stash* me where I'll be safe. I need a mirror. I need room to move. And so do you. We're both going to be miserable."

He shrugged out of his shirt, leaving him in a white T-shirt and khaki pants. T-shirts did nice things for him, or maybe he did nice things for T-shirts. She forced herself to look at his face, rather than the long, lean muscles of his arms and shoulders or the hints of rippled abs hiding under the white cotton.

"If I need something ironed, I go over to Dad's."

Laurel tore her gaze away from his abs. "What? Iron?" She blinked, remembering the dress in her hands. "Oh. Iron."

He sent her an odd look.

She thought about his dad in that big house alone. "I could go over there. In fact, maybe I could stay with your dad," she said. Away from temptation.

He tossed his shirt into the bottom of his closet on top of several others. "Not a chance. I brought you here because trouble seems to follow you around. I'd rather it not follow you to my dad's."

She felt heat creep up from her neck to her face. "I didn't mean—I would never put your father in danger. I just thought it would be nice to have an iron." And be able to stretch my arms without touching you.

He scowled at her. "Don't you have anything else to wear—something that doesn't need ironing?"

She scrutinized the dress again, hoping maybe it wasn't as bad as she'd first thought. But it was a rayon linen blend, and whoever had searched her room had left it in a crumpled heap on the closet floor. It was fatally wrinkled. Not even an iron could help it now.

"I'll figure out something."

Cade turned his head, listening. "The washer's almost done."

"I'll get it." Laurel headed for the bedroom door just as he did. They bumped shoulders as they both tried to go through the door at the same time.

She pulled back and lost her balance. Cade caught her in the nick of time before she took a header over a stack of boxes. She steadied herself against his chest.

"Careful," he said softly. "I can't have you hurting yourself."

By the time she regained her balance, his thumbs were tracing little circles on the sensitive skin inside her elbow. She shivered.

"Why?" she managed. "Are you afraid I'd sue?"

He shook his head and smiled, his blue eyes shimmering like the ocean. "Nope. You're my ticket to the reunion party tonight."

For the first time in her life, Laurel felt a sexual thrill from an innocent touch. But looking into his eyes, she realized it wasn't just a touch—it was the fantasy she'd harbored in her heart since the first time she'd laid eyes on him in high school.

She'd always dreamed that one day he'd walk up to her, pull her into his arms and kiss her.

But it had never happened. Until now.

"Cade?" she whispered.

His thumbs were still caressing her arms. His chest felt as hard and sculpted as it looked. She swallowed. *He was going to kiss her.*

His head dipped toward hers until she could feel his breath fan across her cheek. A voice in her head recited the chronology of events that had led to this moment, and tried to make sense out of them. But how she'd gotten to this point was the last thing she cared about. She just wanted to stay.

Cade slid his hands up her arms and pulled her closer. Just as his lips touched hers, a shrill buzz pierced the air. She jumped and dropped the dress.

"What—?"

Cade's fingers tightened on her arms. "It's just the washing machine. It buzzes when it's done spinning."

Laurel's heart was in her throat. "I'm surprised the neighbors don't complain," she said tightly. "I'll put the clothes in the dryer."

His jaw muscle worked as he let go of her. "I'll shower, then you can have the bathroom all to yourself."

She heard the bathroom door close as she stepped out onto the back porch.

She quickly transferred her now clean lingerie from the washer to the dryer and turned it on.

When she opened the screen door to come back inside, her gaze lit on the mantel over the empty fireplace in Cade's miniscule living room. There were several photos sitting on it.

The shower was still running. *Good.* She had a few minutes to look at his pictures before he came out. Although why she felt the urge to be sneaky she didn't know. They were sitting right there in plain sight. It wasn't like she was digging into his underwear drawer.

Still, her throat fluttered as she surveyed them. There were several, most in inexpensive frames. She picked up one. It was obviously his mother, and obviously a studio portrait. She was pretty, with the same intense blue eyes as Cade. Laurel thought Cade looked a lot like his dad, but she could see from this picture how much he resembled his mother.

When had she died? The picture had a copyright date from twenty years before. Cade would have been around eleven or so.

She put the photo back and picked up one of James. There was no mistaking that wide, charming grin and the cocky, self-assured look in his eyes. Laurel didn't remember ever actually looking into James's eyes, but in the color photograph they were dark—maybe brown.

The next photo was of James with their father. Now *those* two looked alike. Both had dark hair, both had quick, easy grins and both of them had the look of supreme confidence that she'd always associated with James.

Two or three other pictures of James, including one of him in his Air Force uniform sat on the mantel.

"Where are *your* pictures, Cade?" she whispered.

At that very moment, the bathroom door opened and Cade stepped out. He had on sweatpants and a towel was slung around his neck. His hair was wet and spiky and his shoulders sparkled with water droplets. She tore her gaze away from his lean belly and looked down at his bare feet. They stuck out from under the sweat pants—bony, sexy, vulnerable.

He took her breath away.

Picking up the corner of the towel to blot a drop that had caught on his eyelashes, he walked over to her. She could smell the soap and the woodsy rain-fresh scent of his shampoo.

"What are you doing?" he asked shortly.

"Looking at your pictures."

He took the frame from her hands. It was the one of James in his uniform. He studied it for a moment, then set it back on the mantel.

"He was so handsome. I'm really sorry, Cade. I know you must miss him."

He touched each of the pictures in turn, making small adjustments in their positions as if she'd somehow violated them by moving them. "Yeah. I think about him every day."

Laurel's heart twisted painfully. He must have worshipped his older brother. But where were the pictures of *him?* Surely he had photos of himself with James or with his dad.

But she wasn't about to ask. Not right now. Maybe never. She was baffled by the waves of disapproval he sent her way. The pictures were displayed for all to see, yet he didn't want her to touch them.

"You'd better hurry up." He turned his back on her and headed for his bedroom.

She watched him until he disappeared through the door and shut it firmly behind him. Then she fetched her clean underwear from the dryer and headed for the bathroom.

The experience of showering right after him was comforting, disturbing and confusing. The smell of his shampoo permeated the tiny, steam-filled room, sending her imagination into overdrive. She slathered her hair with her own gardenia-scented shampoo, trying to overpower his scent, and did a pretty good job of it.

Without the scent of his shampoo, she almost managed to banish the image of water sluicing over his chest and abs, running down the seductive curve of his back and over his buttocks, between his powerful thighs—

Okay, stop!

Her knees were quivering, her breasts were aching, as were other, deeper parts of her. She wrenched the water tap to cold and bit her lip at the shockingly chill spray.

By the time she finished, she'd managed to turn her thoughts to her clothes. She decided to wear a pair of black pants and a glittery sleeveless top with black high-heeled sandals.

She wrapped herself in the terry cloth robe that hung on the back of the door, popped out long enough to snatch up her clothes, and popped back inside. It took her fifteen minutes to tame her hair.

This time, when she came out, Cade was waiting for her. His hair was still slightly damp. He wore a white dress shirt, gray slacks and a summer-weight sports coat.

"Ready?" he asked shortly.

He was still upset about her touching his pictures. She wished she could figure out why. "Yes."

Just as she spoke, her cell phone rang.

Cade frowned and looked at his watch.

She grabbed her purse and dug in it until she came up with the phone. She didn't recognize the number. "Hello?"

"Laurel? It's Debra Honeycutt."

Laurel sent Cade a surprised look. "Debra? Is something wrong?"

Cade's frown faded and his gaze intensified. He took a step closer and bent his head near her ear until she could feel his breath on her cheek. She tilted the phone slightly so they could both hear.

"I'm so sorry to bother—I need to talk to you." Her voice quavered. She sounded terrified.

"Sure, go ahead."

"No—not now. I can't—"

Laurel heard her suck in a shaky breath.

"Can we—meet some time during the party?"

Cade put his hand on her back and nodded.

"Of course. Where? When? Just tell me and I'll be there."

"There's a side door near the room you used this morning. It leads out—" her voice broke "—out to the path down to the creek."

"You want to meet at the door?"

Debra hesitated an instant. "No. We can't be seen. I want to meet at the creek bank, by the Swinging Oak."

Laurel didn't relish the idea of walking that path in the dark. It was overgrown and who knew what kind of creatures would be scurrying or slithering around in the dark. She looked at Cade questioningly. He nodded again.

"Look, Debra. We can meet now. I'll meet you anywhere."

"It's still light outside. Please—please, Laurel. This is so important. By eight-fifteen or so it'll be dark."

"Okay. Eight-fifteen, then."

"Oh, thank you, thank you. I can't live like this any more. Ten years is just too—"

Debra stopped, and Laurel heard a child crying in the background and a man yelling. Then the phone went dead.

THE REUNION PARTY was everything Laurel expected it to be. People who had never spoken two words to her greeted her like old friends, and girls she'd hung out with barely recognized her. A lot of folks seemed to have no idea what to say to each other, so they loaded their plates with food and kept their mouths full.

Because of the drama surrounding Misty's attack and the fire, or maybe because she was with Cade, she got more than her share of attention. But finally the curiosity waned and she found herself standing near the bar, sipping a glass of chardonnay.

Cade paid the bartender for a beer and then turned to stand beside her. "Do you know all these people?"

"Most of them. There were only sixty or so in our graduating class."

"Got to love small towns."

She wondered at the note of irony in his voice as her gaze swept the crowd.

"Look." She gestured with her glass. "There are Kathy and Mary Sue. And Debra's around here somewhere. Now all they need is Sheryl Posey, and the CeeGees will be reunited." Laurel sipped her wine as she casually observed the two women. "I'd love to hear what they're saying. Have you seen Debra?"

"She brought a plate of sandwiches in from the kitchen about twenty minutes ago." Cade turned his beer bottle up and drank.

"Here she comes."

Debra hung back from the other two women until Kathy turned and spoke to her. Kathy pointed toward the

DJ's table, then headed in that direction. Debra meekly followed behind her while Mary Sue wandered off through the crowd.

Kathy stopped in front of the DJ's speakers, the one place in the room where they wouldn't be overheard.

Kathy was obviously angry. Debra pinched her lips together and looked miserable.

"They're arguing," Laurel said. "Do you think she found out Debra called me?"

Cade shrugged. "No telling. Knowing Kathy, she could be upset because Debra brought out a hundred sandwiches instead of a hundred and fifty."

"You don't think Debra has any information for me, do you? I think she does. She said *ten years is too*—something. Probably *too long*. I think she was saying that she wants to come clean about something from ten years ago. I think she knows what happened to Wendell."

He shrugged. "Could be. I'm sure she's got something she feels is important, but I wouldn't count on it being a big revelation. Debra can be a little excitable. Her husband was late getting home from a business trip several months ago, and she couldn't reach his cell phone. She wanted me to alert every highway patrolman between here and St. Louis."

Laurel was still watching the two CeeGees. Kathy snapped at Debra. Debra backed away, then turned and ran. At the same time, the hired DJ tapped his microphone and started his spiel about popular hits from a decade before.

Kathy glared at him as if he'd interrupted her. He ignored her, so she stomped away.

Laurel looked back at Cade. "So was Debra's husband okay?"

"He showed up within the hour. Said he'd had a flat tire, and his cell phone battery had run down."

"That might fit with Ann Noble's revelation about their affair. Maybe he *was* with her or another woman."

Cade looked skeptical.

"Still, I can't take the chance. She might really know something," Laurel said.

"Speaking of Ann Noble," Cade replied, "have you seen her tonight?"

"No." Laurel frowned. "I haven't. That's odd."

"Did she say she'd be at the reunion?"

"I just assumed she'd be here, since she was on the committee. But no. I don't think she ever said."

At that moment, music filled the air—a power ballad that everyone recognized, and the lights dimmed and shimmered with color.

A plump, pretty redhead walked up and asked Cade about Misty. She was the latest in a stream of women who'd found a reason to talk to him ever since they'd arrived.

"She's doing fine. Her parents came in from Florida today. They're taking her back with them for a visit."

Laurel watched him. Just like every other time, he was polite, friendly and attentive.

His smile produced a blush more times than not, but his body language sent a different message. He stood balanced on the balls of his feet with his arms crossed. He didn't bend toward any of the women. He kept his back straight.

The redhead smiled and made a little small talk, but after a couple of silent nods from him, she spoke to Laurel and then drifted away.

Laurel chuckled quietly and took another sip of wine.

"What are you laughing at?"

She shook her head. "I wasn't laughing. I was just thinking how different you are from your brother."

A grimace flashed across his face, reminding her of the

way he'd looked when he found her with James's picture in her hand.

"Oh, my gosh, Cade. That was a really stupid remark. I didn't mean to bring up painful memories. I'm so sorry."

"Forget it." He set his beer bottle down and held out his hand to her. "Dance with me."

"What?" She stared at his hand. "I—I suck at dancing."

"Well, I don't. Come on. I'll cover for you."

She sent him a withering glance. "Thanks," she said, "but I'm supposed to meet Debra in a few minutes."

"In eleven minutes." He took her hand and led her out onto the dance floor. A few other couples were already there, including Kathy and Ralph Langston. Kathy misstepped and laughed shrilly.

"Look at them," Laurel whispered. "Kathy's laughing, but she looks scared. And look at how tightly Ralph is holding her. Do you think he's hurting her?"

At that moment, Kathy broke away from Ralph and stumbled. She looked around, spotted her husband who was standing at the bar and headed his way.

Ralph straightened his tie and made a ridiculous spectacle of walking casually off the dance floor.

"Don't worry about them," Cade said as he pulled her into his arms and took her right hand in his left. "Now I've got you," he whispered in her ear. "What differences between James and me?"

Laurel's heart pounded. She tried to hold her body away from his, afraid he'd feel her pulse hammering. But he held her close. "I said I was sorry. It was a thoughtless comment."

"James has been dead a long time, but people still talk about him. It doesn't bother me."

She leaned back and looked at him. "But—"

"But what?"

"Nothing." She shook her head. He was lying. It *did* bother him. Twice already she'd witnessed the pain that flickered across his face when his brother's name was mentioned. Why was he so quick to deny his feelings? It obviously hurt him to talk about James.

"I'm not letting you go until you tell me what you meant."

His palm slid along the waistband of her pants. "Hey, where's your weapon, Special Agent Gillespie?"

"It's—" she croaked. "It's in my purse."

He bent his head again and his breath was warm on her ear as he whispered, "Well, be sure you can get to it if you need it."

She closed her eyes against the feeling of his lips so close to her ear. She nodded.

He spread his fingers and slid his palm down to rest just above the curve of her bottom. Her mouth went dry.

"Now, you were about to tell me the difference between James and me."

"Hmm? Oh." She cleared her throat. "I was watching how you handled those women."

He gave her a glimpse of his crooked smile. "*Handled* them?"

Her cheeks heated up, just like one of them. She swallowed with an effort. "You aim that killer smile at each one and make her feel like she's the only person in your world—in that way you're like James. But the whole time you're charming a woman with your smile and your eyes, your body language is sending a different message. *I'm doing my job. Don't linger.*"

His smile turned quizzical and he looked down between them without missing a step. "Is that what my body is saying?"

"Well, not right now—" She clamped her mouth shut. Oh, my. Had she said that aloud?

"Oh, yeah? What's it saying right now?" he drawled. His hand on her back pressed a little harder. She could feel the brush of his thighs against her, and his crisp white shirt scraping against her breasts was titillating and painful at the same time. She knew she'd regret wearing the little jeweled silk top with no jacket. Her breasts tightened against the thin material.

"Laurel?" He pressed his cheek against her temple and his lips brushed her ear. "Come on. You started this. What's my body saying?"

She took a shaky breath. "You know what I meant."

"Do I?"

Suddenly she realized the music had changed and nobody but the two of them were still holding each other. She stopped in the middle of the dance floor and pushed him away. "I need to—go find Debra." She glanced around at the people dancing to the driving rhythm of a metal-rock song. "What time is it?"

He led her off the dance floor. "It's been thirteen minutes," he whispered in her ear.

"Thirteen? I'm two minutes late. Debra will be frantic. What are you going to do?"

"What do you think? I'm going to follow you."

"Well, don't get too close. If Debra hears or sees you she's liable to bolt."

He gave her a brief nod. "I'm heading out the front door. I'll circle around, and yes, I'll stay hidden."

She glanced sidelong at him. "Good. Thanks."

Laurel exited through the side door onto a concrete landing. A couple of sconces lit a half circle about two feet in diameter, but beyond that the area was cloaked in darkness.

She glanced to the left and right. There were similar sconces every twenty feet along the side of the building. The front of the building facing the parking lot was brightly lit. Several people stood around smoking and talking.

Debra had been right about the side door. It directly faced the old path that led down to the creek bank. Down to the Swinging Oak where the rope hung—where Wendell had been found. Laurel stood just inside the circle of light for a few seconds but nobody seemed to notice her. She checked the time on her cell phone. 8:19.

She'd expected Debra to stay close to the building. Even though she'd said she wanted to meet down by the creek bank, Laurel pegged her for the type who'd be afraid of the dark.

But maybe she was wrong. If Debra hadn't chickened out completely, then she was already on the path to the creek. Laurel had to get going.

The air was heavy and smelled like rain as she started toward the path. Above her the sky was a deep gray. Below, the ground was damp and slick.

As she moved farther away from the Visitor Center, the darkness intensified. She had a flashlight in her purse beside her weapon, but she didn't want to attract attention. She moved forward slowly, waiting for her eyes to adapt to the dark.

The moon peeked out from behind a cloud just as she stepped onto the path that decades of horny high-school kids had beaten. It was at the edge of the area that had been cleared for the new convention complex.

The moonlight helped, but the trees cast dense shadows and the heels of her sandals kept catching in roots and vines.

Behind her she could hear the faint sounds of the DJ's music. In front of her, she heard water.

The creek. She was almost there. Almost to the small clearing on the creek bank where Wendell had died. She suppressed a little shiver.

Don't be such a wimp, Gillespie.

So what if Wendell had died down here? She wasn't superstitious, nor was she a fraidy cat. The night, the situation and the specter of murder were just slightly creepy.

A twig snapped behind her. She froze and slid her hand into her purse. The chill of the steel reassured her. She wrapped her fingers around the handle of her little Smith & Wesson.

"Debra?" she whispered.

Only silence greeted her.

She waited a few seconds, but nothing moved. There wasn't even a breeze to stir the trees. The utter silence was eerie—unnatural.

Suddenly, she heard footsteps to her left. Her fingers tightened around her gun as she swung it toward the sound.

"Who's there?"

Chapter Seven

Cade heard Laurel call out. He was twenty paces behind her and although her pale bare shoulders were easy to see even in the dark, twenty paces was too far. He didn't know what Debra's game was, but someone was targeting Laurel. Whoever it was, *he* was targeting them.

Trees rustled and twigs crunched just a few feet away. He swung his weapon, but he couldn't see anyone. Was it Debra? Had she chickened out and run away?

He didn't think so. The crunching told him the person was bigger and heavier than Debra. The footsteps sounded stealthy, rather than panicked.

He turned his full attention back to Laurel. She slipped almost silently through the thickening underbrush. He liked the way she moved. She didn't waste time or energy on swaying her hips or swinging her hair. He appreciated that. He'd never been impressed by women who flaunted their bodies or their looks.

Laurel's femininity and strength were apparent in the shape of her small, compact body. The curve of her shoulders, the gentle swell of her biceps and the firmness of her triceps. As he traced her slow advance, he thought about how silky and firm her shoulders had felt under his hands and how supple and sexy her body had felt pressed against his as they danced.

She stopped and cocked her head, as if listening to something he hadn't heard. Then she started forward again.

An instant later she was gone.

Laurel! Cade's heart crashed against his chest wall. One second she was there and the next—

His first instinct was to surge forward yelling her name. But he had to stay quiet. If someone had attacked her, the only thing he had on his side was surprise.

Had Debra's call been a trap? Cade slid his weapon out of his holster and eased forward, all his senses concentrated on the last place he'd seen her.

He was thankful for the cloak of darkness, but he wished the moon would come out again. He needed just one split-second of light to get his bearings.

As if granting his wish, the moon peeked out from behind a cloud, lending pale light and sinister shadows to the overgrown area where Laurel had disappeared.

He held his breath and waited, while his nerves screamed and his muscles cramped. Then his eyes caught a shadowy flicker that was out of sync—moving in the wrong direction. He swung his weapon toward it, just as he heard a quiet gasp.

"Oh, God, Debra!"

Laurel. He had no time to chase shadows. Gripping his gun in both hands, he headed toward Laurel's voice. Silvery moonlight lay like a layer of dust over two figures on the ground.

"Laurel?"

She started and twisted around. "Cade?" Her eyes glittered in the pale moonlight. "Oh, Cade, she's dead."

"Are you sure?" He swept the area around them with his

gaze, his ears tuned to any odd sound. But everything seemed quiet. Shifting his stance, he dug a small, high-powered flashlight out of his pocket.

She nodded. "No pulse."

Her voice was shaky but calm. He was sure she'd seen her share of dead bodies in her job, but this was different. Even if she hadn't liked Debra, she'd known her.

Cade crouched beside her. "Did you see anything? Hear anything?"

"I tripped over her." Anguish laced her voice.

Cade shone the flashlight's beam on Debra's face.

"Look at her, Cade. Her face, her lips." She carefully lifted an eyelid. "Petechial hemorrhaging. She was strangled."

Cade nodded as helpless anger burned in his chest. Debra didn't deserve this. She'd been trying to help.

"May I see your flashlight?" she asked.

He handed it to her and watched as she swept the light across every inch of Debra's face and neck.

"Check out her neck," he said. "The bruising."

She nodded. "I think her hyoid bone is broken."

"Just like Wendell."

Laurel met his gaze, her eyes wide and filled with horror. "Just like Wendell," she whispered.

IT WAS WELL after midnight by the time Cade had rounded up all the reunion party guests, gotten the medical examiner down from Three Springs to pronounce Debra dead and cordoned off the crime scene.

Laurel began questioning the guests while he processed the scene. The editor of the weekly Dusty Springs newspaper had been recording the reunion activities, so Laurel had him set up his video camera to record her interrogations for the record.

Once the medical examiner had left to transport Debra's body back to Three Springs for an autopsy, Cade did a preliminary walk-through of the crime scene. He found Laurel's purse with her gun still in it. But the moon stayed behind the clouds, and rain started to fall. Cade had to respect the fine balance between preserving evidence and trampling all over any clues in the dark. He left Shelton guarding the crime scene and came in to see how the questioning was progressing.

As he approached the small conference room in the Visitor Center, Mary Sue Nelson breezed out the door. She gave him a flirtatious smile, then laid her hand on his arm and transformed her face into earnest sadness.

"How tragic," she said. "Poor Debra. I suppose you know her husband was having an affair."

Cade shifted slightly—just enough to get away from her touch. "Oh?" he said noncommittally. "Did you tell Laurel—Special Agent Gillespie?"

"Why, I don't remember." Mary Sue dug in her purse and came up with a crisply folded tissue. She touched the corners of her eyes. "I'm so distraught. I just can't believe she's gone."

Cade pushed open the conference room door.

Laurel had leaned back in her chair and was twisting her hair up into a knot at the back of her head. She let it go and its wispy ends framed her face softly. Then she arched her neck.

"Long night," Cade said.

She nodded as she rubbed her eyes. "Long weekend. And I have a feeling it's going to get longer."

Cade acknowledged the newspaper editor with a nod. "Dave, thanks for staying and taping the interviews. You know not to tell anyone what you heard."

"Sure thing, Cade. Want me to leave the camera?"

He looked at Laurel who shook her head. "I think we've talked to everyone."

"You know, I never did see Kathy Adler," Dave said.

Laurel scanned her list. "No, but her husband said she'd gone home."

"Okay." Dave yawned. "See you tomorrow."

After he left, Cade turned to Laurel. "What do you think about Kathy disappearing?"

She shook her head. "You saw her. She was already tipsy at the beginning of the party. In that state I don't think she could have overpowered Debra and strangled her. But we definitely need to talk to her as soon as possible."

"So what about the others?" Laurel rubbed her temples with her fingertips. "You know, any of our usual suspects could have killed Debra."

Cade bit off a curse. "What do you mean?"

"The DJ lowered the lights once the dancing started."

"Yeah," he said. He remembered being glad the lights were dim while he was holding her in his arms on the dance floor. That memory stirred his libido and he had to force his gaze away from the delicate shadow between her breasts.

"Everybody seems to have developed night blindness. Not a single person remembered any of our suspects being in the room during that time."

"Langston?"

She shook her head. "Swears he never left the room. But he wouldn't name anyone specific he was with. The only time I remember seeing him is when he was dancing with Kathy. I was deliberately watching people and I can't tell you whether anyone disappeared before I left to meet Debra."

"What about the couples? Didn't they vouch for each other?"

"Sure. Most of the guests didn't seem to have a clue what was going on. But our usual suspects were careful not to implicate anyone—or alibi anyone. So we have no witnesses. The only one who has an airtight alibi is Debra's husband. He was in a conversation with the DJ about music during the time she was killed." She rubbed her temples again. "All we have to rely on is physical evidence."

"Well, we may have solved one mystery."

"Really? What?"

"Debra was missing a fake fingernail."

Laurel sat up straight. "A French nail?"

He frowned and shrugged.

"They have white tips," she said. "Like the one I found in my room."

"I don't know. I already gave it to the ME."

"Which hand?"

"Right."

Laurel shook her head. "I can't believe it was Debra who broke into my room."

"Is it easier to believe she could knock Misty out and leave her there?"

"No. I can't imagine her doing *anything* sneaky or violent. Not to mention the skill it would have taken to pick that lock at the B&B."

The bed-and-breakfast—of course. "Hang on a minute," he said. "Maybe she didn't have to break in. Holder is Fred's brother-in-law. I'd forgotten that. Fred's sister died several years ago, but Debra could have gotten a key from her uncle."

"Well, we'll know when we get the ME's photos. You did tell him to photograph the hand with the missing nail, didn't you?"

"I went one better. I got some instant shots. I keep a camera in my pickup."

"You took pictures?"

She didn't have to look so surprised that he'd followed basic procedure and taken crime-scene photos. He opened his mouth but she obviously read the irritation on his face.

"Sorry. Of course you did."

He pulled the small stack of photos out of his shirt pocket.

Laurel took them. As she spread them out on the table he stepped behind her and leaned over. When he did, her evocative gardenia scent assaulted his nostrils. Damn, did she have to smell so good? Forcing himself not to press his nose against her hair, he pulled back an inch or so.

"There's the shot of her hand." He pointed over her shoulder. "I need to get a digital camera, but right now this is the best I can do."

"It's good enough. Her nails are pink, not French."

"I thought you said they all had the French ones."

"They did. Debra must have had hers redone sometime today." She sat back and her hair brushed Cade's cheek. Gardenias whirled around his head, just like when he and she were dancing. He straightened and stepped away. Another few seconds and he'd be looking for a cold shower. He cursed under his breath. He had to do something to stop this ridiculous and extremely inconvenient physical attraction to her.

He spoke through gritted teeth. "So it could still be hers. I guess she'd have to redo them if she lost one?"

She sighed. "We have to rely on the DNA." She gathered up the photos and handed them back to him.

He nodded toward the video camera. "Any decent info on that thing? An eyewitness? A confession?" He was kidding—sort of.

She sent him an ironic glance. "At least three people told

me in strictest confidence that George Honeycutt is having an affair. Nobody knows who with, and everybody is sure Debra knew about it."

"What did Honeycutt say?"

Laurel squeezed her eyes shut and shook her head. "He seemed genuinely broken up. In shock. Almost as devastated as her dad."

"Yeah, I talked to Fred while the ME was working on her. He said she'd been upset about something. When he asked her about it, she told him everything was okay, that she was stressed out about the upcoming reunion."

"I asked George if she'd seemed upset or worried and he said she was always upset about one thing or another."

"Did you ask him about Ann Noble?"

She nodded. "He seemed shocked. Said he barely knew her. He appeared to be telling the truth."

"I'll check with Fred. He never liked his son-in-law. He always complained that George was too controlling."

"Controlling?"

"According to him, George didn't want Debra to leave the house at all without him."

"That could be ominous. Makes me wonder how she managed to get away during the party. We should go over his interview together. His answers were pat. Maybe too pat. I want to study his body language." She pushed a strand of hair behind her ear. "How is Fred holding up? I only saw him for a few seconds."

"She was his only child. Her mother died a few years ago."

"Poor Fred."

Cade assessed Laurel. She looked like she was about to collapse. Her hands were shaky and her face was pale.

"Speaking of holding up—what about you?"

Laurel's jaw tightened and she looked down at her

hands. "I'm fine. I shouldn't have let Debra go out there by herself. I should have insisted that we meet before the party, or made her talk to me on the phone."

"You couldn't have known what was going to happen. You can't blame yourself. She must have told someone that she was meeting you."

"Or someone saw her leave and followed her. I heard footsteps running past me just before I tripped over her body."

"Yeah, I heard them, too."

"Did you see anything?"

"It was too dark. But it sounded like a man. Too much noise for a woman."

"So what next? Roust Kathy out of bed and grill her?"

He shook his head. "I don't think there's anything else we can do tonight. You haven't had a full night's sleep since you got here. I say we turn in and start fresh in the morning."

"We should go over the interviews."

"We will. But not tonight."

Laurel rubbed her face and twisted her hair up. "Aren't you concerned that the person who killed Debra will run off—or worse, go after someone else?"

Cade spoke through gritted teeth. "Yes. But what do you suggest I do about it? Put everybody in town in jail?"

"No, of course not." Her cheeks turned pink. "But what if the killer runs?"

"Then we'll know who he is, because everybody else will still be here."

She sent him a withering look.

Cade shrugged, then picked up the video camera and opened the door.

With a sigh, Laurel stood and followed him out into the empty main lobby of the Visitor Center.

"What about Ann Noble?" he asked as he held the exit

door open for her and then led the way to his pickup. "She never showed up. Nobody mentioned her?"

Laurel shook her head. "Nobody. I asked Ralph where she was but he acted like he was the last person in town who would know her whereabouts."

"I wish we could find someone who's seen them together," Cade said.

"Me, too. Ann says she's sleeping with George Honeycutt. George denies it, and Ralph would rather leave himself without an alibi than betray his 'unnamed lady friend.' So who do you think is lying?"

Cade reached around her to open the door. "All of them."

LAUREL SNUGGLED DEEPER into the handmade quilt Cade had given her and squeezed her eyes shut, trying to pretend the light shining in through the window wasn't the sun. No such luck.

It had taken her forever to get to sleep the night before. It was after 2:00 a.m. when they'd gotten back to Cade's house. Then they'd argued over where she would sleep. She'd won that round. There was no way she'd have gotten one wink of sleep lying in Cade's bed while he tried to fold his long body onto the couch.

He'd finally relented and given her a quilt and a pillow, still grumbling about her stubbornness.

When he'd come out of the bathroom, she'd caught a glimpse of him in his dress pants and no shirt. She'd listened to him moving around in the bedroom while her brain turned each sound into a video. She heard him kick off his shoes, heard the soft sound of fabric sliding along skin—his pants.

Then a drawer opened and closed, and she heard more fabric rustling, and finally, the quiet creak of bedsprings when he got into bed.

Her mind had obsessed over what he wore to bed. He'd gotten something out of a drawer. Boxer shorts? Pajama bottoms? Another pair of those sexy gray sweatpants?

She'd groaned quietly as a bone-melting thrill streaked through to her core and reminded her of how safe, how sexy, how feminine she'd felt when they'd danced. *Argh!*

She'd stuck her head under the covers that smelled like him, and forced herself to think about Debra's murder. The concentration it required to mentally trace the steps of the killer had settled her mind and she'd finally fallen to sleep.

And now, too few hours later, the sun was getting brighter, defying her attempts to ignore it. She stuck her nose out from under the quilt and squinted at the window, then sat up and reached for her purse. Groping inside, she finally closed her fist around her cell phone. She looked at the display. Seven o'clock.

She groaned.

A movement caught the edge of her vision. Cade stood in his bedroom doorway in the sweatpants she'd fantasized about. They rode low on his hips. His upper body was bare, as were his feet. The early morning sunlight dusted his skin with gold as he rubbed his chest and yawned, then pushed his fingers through his tousled hair.

"D'you sleep okay?" His voice was soft and rough.

Trying to pretend that seeing him warm and sleepy, just out of bed wasn't turning her on, she shrugged. "Pretty well considering."

She sank back down onto the couch and pulled the quilt up over her breasts. Her satin pajamas were fairly modest but she still felt self-conscious, especially considering the sexually charged intimacy of their situation.

"I told you to take the bed."

"It wasn't that. It was just—everything."

He clamped his jaw. "I know. Need the bathroom?"

She shook her head. "Go ahead."

By the time he came out, she'd taken a quick tour of the kitchen, rinsed out the coffeepot, found a can of coffee in the freezer and brewed a pot.

"Wow." Cade rounded the corner between the bathroom and the kitchen. He grinned as she handed him a full mug.

"What a great way to wake up. Coming straight out of the shower to a hot cup of coffee."

She looked at him over the brim of her cup. "Your coffeemaker has a timer on it."

He shook his head. "That's too much trouble. I like this method better."

She squeezed the cup tightly and did her best not to melt under his killer grin. Was he *flirting* with her?

Enough of that, she lectured herself silently. "So I guess we'd better get going. Do you mind if I take a shower?"

"Not a bit." His gaze left her face and traveled down the front of her satin pajamas. She'd have sworn she felt them dissolving under his heated gaze. Why did she ever think they were modest?

"Let me know if you need any help." When he met her gaze again, she was shocked to see raw hunger there. Then his mouth widened slowly into an innocent smile.

Heaven help her, he *was* flirting with her. She set her cup carefully on the counter, working hard not to smile. "I think I can manage."

She glanced toward the bathroom. She was going to have to squeeze past him to get out from behind the counter. She waited for him to step aside, but he didn't. He just stood there.

With a glare, she rounded the corner of the counter. At

the very last second, he stepped aside enough that only her shoulder brushed his bare chest.

She couldn't look at him. "What's first on the agenda this morning?" She tossed the question over her shoulder.

"I wish it wasn't Sunday. I'm ready to officially request the FBI's help."

Her heart leaped as she turned. He did believe she could help him—unless he was going to request another agent. "Help with Debra's death, or with Wendell's case?"

"Both."

"And you want to request me."

He nodded.

"We can call my boss, Mitch Decker. He can authorize my official presence on the case. Want to talk to him now while I shower?"

"Sure. It's not too early?"

She grabbed her phone. "He and his wife have a new baby. He's probably been up for hours already."

Sure enough, when Mitch answered his phone, Laurel could hear the baby crying.

"Mitch, hi. Sounds like you're having a great morning."

"Morning, Laurel. Joelle is teething, so she's grouchy and her mom and dad are sleep-deprived. What about you? Aren't you supposed to be having fun at your high-school reunion weekend?"

"Mitch, I'm going to put you on the phone with Cade Dupree. He's the chief of police here in Dusty Springs. A woman was murdered at the reunion party last night. Cade would like to ask for the FBI's help."

"Are you all right?"

"I'm fine."

"That's good. So how does this woman's murder fall under our purview?"

"We think it's connected to an apparent suicide from ten years ago." She met Cade's gaze, hoping he wouldn't contradict her. He *did* say he was including Wendell's death.

"*Apparent* suicide?"

"A boy from my graduating class was found hanged on graduation night ten years ago. But I think he was murdered and the murdered woman knew something about it. She was waiting to meet with me when the killer struck."

Chapter Eight

"Your boss thinks a lot of you," Cade said, shifting his pickup out of reverse.

"I think a lot of him. Mitch Decker is the most honorable man I've ever known. He won't accept anything less than a hundred percent effort, and he gives two hundred percent himself. Any one of his agents would take a bullet for him."

"Sounds like a good place to work."

Laurel heard an odd note in Cade's voice. Almost a wistfulness. He'd trained at Quantico and had just received his first assignment when his brother died and his dad had a stroke.

Did he wish he'd followed through and become a special agent? Was he jealous of her for achieving what he hadn't? She wanted to tell him that he could still go back to the FBI. It wouldn't be easy, but it was possible.

She knew he'd originally returned to Dusty Springs because of his dad, but why had he stayed? She hated this town, but her perspective was skewed. Maybe he loved it. Somehow, even as she thought the words, she knew they didn't ring true.

"Why did you resign your position with the FBI? You could have taken bereavement leave when your brother died." She'd come to expect the tense bulge of his jaw when she said something he didn't like. And there it went. She almost smiled.

"My dad had a stroke."

"But that was five years ago."

He didn't say anything. He threw up a barrier that might as well have been visible, it was so palpable.

Giving up for the moment, she looked out the window. "I thought we were going back to the crime scene."

"You're going to the office. You can go over the evidence we got last night and review Wendell Vance's case file. See what Dad thought at the time." He sounded a little too casual.

"And you? Where are you going?"

"The crime scene."

"Oh, no. Not by yourself. I'm going, too."

He cut his eyes over at her. "I guess you noticed it rained again during the night. You're hardly dressed to crawl around in the mud."

"Jeans and running shoes?"

"Designer jeans and brand new running shoes."

"Don't worry about my clothes. I've crawled through the mud in a miniskirt before."

Cade muttered something. It took her a second to figure out what he'd said. *I'd pay real money to see that.*

"You don't have that much money," she murmured.

He laughed. "Maybe we could barter."

Laurel's cheeks grew warm and a sweet yearning built inside her. It was still hard for her to believe that he was flirting with her. Too bad she'd flunked flirting in junior high, she thought wryly. Still, it was fun to banter with him. "What could you possibly have that I'd want?"

"Oh, I don't know. I could probably *come up* with something."

Suddenly everything he said sounded like a double entendre to her. She was pathetic. Get a grip, Gillespie. This was a collaboration on a murder investigation, not a date.

"Okay, Dupree. I'm officially on the case now, so I'm going with you to the crime scene." He didn't argue, didn't even look at her. He just turned the pickup around. Within five minutes, they were turning onto the road to the Visitor Center. He parked at the edge of the pavement.

The section of the path where Laurel had found Debra's body was several yards south of the Visitor Center, only a few feet from the clearing where the Swinging Oak leaned over the creek.

Cade and Laurel trudged over a slight rise and looked down over the overgrown area that surrounded the creek. Part of it had been flattened by bulldozers in preparation for building the convention complex. But the crime scene was farther—along the path through the overgrown area.

They passed the digging and grading equipment—abandoned on Sunday morning, and two vehicles, one a dark green SUV, the other a sporty Lexus.

Cade grunted.

"You know those cars?"

"Yeah." He sounded disgusted.

Just then, they topped the rise that looked down on the spot where Debra was murdered.

"Ah, hell," Cade muttered.

"What you said," Laurel growled.

There were two people standing just to the side of the crime-scene tape—two irritatingly familiar people. Ralph Langston and Kathy Adler. And they appeared to be arguing.

"Where's Officer Phillips?"

"I told him he could leave around seven or so. That I'd be out here early."

Cade lengthened his stride. "Hey!"

Laurel ran to keep up. The soles of her brand-new running shoes sank into the mud.

"Cade. Laurel." Ralph greeted them as if they were sitting in a coffee shop, not trespassing on the scene of a brutal crime.

"Have you been inside the barricade?" Laurel snapped.

Ralph sent her an amused look. "No, ma'am. Although as barricades go, this one is pretty flimsy."

"What are you doing here, Langston?" Cade moved a step closer to him.

Kathy stepped closer to Ralph. "We were discussing the idea of erecting a memorial to Debra on this spot."

Laurel caught the look Ralph shot Kathy's way.

"A what?" Cade waved a hand. "Never mind. I heard you. First of all, this is a crime scene. Nobody is going to do anything here until I release it. Second, it's barely been twelve hours since she was murdered. I think a *memorial* could wait a few days." His fists were clenched and his stance was commanding, maybe even aggressive. "And third, I wouldn't be too hasty to make plans if I were you. Once we've uncovered the killer, you might not be so anxious to have an eternal reminder of the murder."

Kathy gasped.

Langston's face turned red with anger. "Is that an accusation, *Chief Dupree?*"

"Not at all. Merely a warning." Cade took another step forward. "Now you two should get away from here. We've got work to do. And Langston—call off your heavy equipment until I release the crime scene."

"You're shutting me down? You can't do that. The convention complex has got to be finished. I've got a schedule."

"Not anymore. Now go home."

"This is my property," Langston groused.

"And my crime scene. I'll get a court order if I have to."

Kathy propped her fists on her hips and glared at Cade and then at Laurel. "Why does *she* get to stay?"

"Because *she* is an FBI special agent. She'll be working with me on Debra's murder."

"FBI? You? That was the little badge you were waving around? It's Laura or something like that, isn't it?"

"Something like that," Laurel said. She leveled a gaze at the former *Cool Girl*. Kathy was in the same outfit she'd worn to the party the night before. The dress was wrinkled and her high-heeled sandals were covered with mud. She looked like she hadn't been to sleep at all. She also looked like she'd been drinking all night.

Kathy glanced at Ralph, then Cade. "Why didn't somebody tell me she was an FBI agent?" she asked.

"Somebody did. Several times," Cade said flatly.

"Come on, Kathy, let's leave the cops to do their job." Ralph put a hand on the small of Kathy's back. Given their argument and Kathy's faintly apprehensive expression, Laurel suspected Ralph's touch was more of a warning than a gentlemanly gesture.

"Don't go too far, Kathy," Cade said. "You disappeared during the questioning last night. Where were you?"

"I—wasn't feeling well. I left early and went home to bed."

"Shelton will contact you," Cade said. "There are questions we need you to answer."

Kathy shot Laurel a cutting look as she stalked away.

As soon as the two topped the rise heading back toward the Visitor Center, Cade held up the crime-scene tape for Laurel to slip under. He handed her a pair of rubber gloves and a few small evidence bags.

"Who knows if we'll find anything, but if we do, at least we'll be prepared."

Laurel nodded as she stuck the bags in her pocket and pulled on the gloves. She studied the scene. In the daylight, it looked just like it had felt the night before.

Overgrown, the path littered with roots and vines, leaves and twigs. In the daylight, Laurel could see the end of the path where it opened out into the clearing at the creek bank. She could see the sun dancing on the water in the creek and the dark shadow of the rope fragment that hung from the branch of the Swinging Oak like a broken noose. She shuddered.

"Laurel?"

"She was almost there. Another ten feet or so and Debra would have made it to the clearing. I didn't realize we were so close." Ten more feet and it might have been harder for the killer to sneak up on her, Laurel realized.

"I followed the path as well as I could. Even in the dark I could tell that someone had recently gone the same way. Most of the raindrops had already been knocked off the leaves." She moved slowly forward.

"About right here I heard someone headed back that way. Toward the Visitor Center. They were trying to be quiet, but I could tell it was a human. He or she was about three feet or so to my left."

She stopped. "And right here is where I tripped over Debra."

"Wait a minute. Raindrops?" Cade was right behind her. "It had rained earlier. Did you have trouble walking? What kind of shoes did you have on?"

Laurel sighed. "Black sandals."

"Like Debra's. We bagged them. They were covered with mud. What did you do with yours?"

"I left them on your front stoop. I'm sure they're ruined.

And then it rained again in the night. Looks like whatever physical evidence you picked up last night is all we're going to get."

He was still looking at her feet.

"What are you thinking?"

"Kathy's feet."

She assessed him. "You're right. Kathy had on the same clothes she wore last night. Were those the same shoes? I can't remember."

"Don't look at me."

"We need her shoes. We might be able to detect two different samples of mud on them."

"It'll be tough to prove she was out here last night, but it would certainly give her something to explain. I'll get Shelton to get her shoes first. Then he can go back and check everybody else's."

Laurel turned her attention to the ground where Debra was found. She took her flashlight and shone it slowly across the crushed leaves and grass, not really expecting to find anything. Still she had to look. She owed it to Debra to figure out who killed her.

"So how do you deal with situations like this? If you only have two officers, what happens when you have a major case?"

Cade pulled a flashlight out of his pocket and began scanning the opposite side of the cordoned-off area. "We don't have major cases. This is the first death by foul play we've had since—hell, since Wendell's suicide."

Something caught Laurel's eye. She crouched down. "Cade. Look here. It's a pink fingernail, or at least part of it."

He skirted the area they hadn't yet searched and came up behind her. She stood so he could crouch down and look at it.

"Debra's missing nail. It's broken."

"I know. I don't see the missing piece anywhere. It wasn't on her?"

"We'll have to wait to hear back from the ME. But I searched her clothes and the ground right around her. This is—" he looked around "—what—three feet from where she was found?"

"Have you got your camera? We need to get a photo of this before I bag it."

"It's in the pickup. Let's go get it."

She shook her head. "You go. I don't want to take a chance of losing this. Who knows who else might come wandering around. What if the other piece of her nail is caught in the killer's clothes? It could turn out to be the vital piece of evidence that convicts the murderer."

"Here." He pulled a small plastic marker from his pocket. "Mark the place."

"Thanks. Why don't you go get the camera? It'll take you two minutes. I don't want to leave the scene unattended. What if Ralph or Kathy comes back?"

Cade scowled at her. "I'll be right back." He stood and carefully made his way out of the cordoned-off area.

Laurel crouched down again, slowly sweeping the area around the broken nail with the flashlight beam. She bent close to the ground to look under leaves and in between blades of grass.

There. Under some scattered leaves. She started to brush them aside, but she didn't want to chance disturbing the nail fragments.

Standing, she reached into the back pocket of her jeans for the miniature pad and pen she always carried. She could use the pen to carefully lift the leaf without disturbing anything else.

Something hit the tree trunk right beside her head. She dropped instinctively just as another thud echoed and two quick reports reached her ears.

Gunshots! Someone was shooting at her.

She drew her weapon and rolled up into a crouch. She glanced up at the tree, trying to judge the trajectory of the bullet. She felt a brush of air on her cheek as the bullet whizzed past. She touched her cheek then looked at her fingertip. Nothing. No blood.

She heard a shout. She rose up enough to see Cade crown the top of the rise, his weapon clutched in both hands. He looked like a movie hero, his powerful legs pumping, his torso undulating like a sprinter as he ran toward the direction the bullet had come from.

She rose and aimed her gun, but saw nothing. She carefully ducked under the crime-scene tape and loped up the hill.

Cade waved her back, but she wasn't about to hide while he went after the lowlife who'd shot at her. By the time she reached his side, he'd lowered his gun. He stood, feet planted apart, his fists on his hips, his chest heaving. Sweat shone on his face and glistened on his bare arms.

"Did you see anything?" she panted.

He shook his head. "He stood somewhere around here. The sun's hot today, so the ground up here is already dry. No footprints." He pointed toward the southwest. "Take a look down there. Whoever did it had a perfect shot."

Laurel looked back down the hill. The yellow crime-scene tape stood out in sharp contrast to the grass and foliage surrounding it. She glanced down at her orange T-shirt, which must have shone like a banner, then back toward the crime scene.

She raised her weapon and aimed at the spot where she'd stood just a few minutes ago. The idea of someone standing where she now stood and aiming a gun at her was profoundly disturbing. But she couldn't think about that. She was a professional, and she could never let Cade see how much being shot at had spooked her.

In a show of bravado that was as much for herself as for Cade she pointed her weapon, pursed her lips and made a childish mock sound of a gun firing.

Cade reached over and wrapped his fingers around her gun's barrel and pushed it down.

"He stood up here in plain sight." She scanned the horizon and traced the line of trees and tangled undergrowth that hid the creek. The water had etched a sharp curve—almost a horseshoe—into the landscape over the years. The swimming hole and the Swinging Oak were located right at the curve of the horseshoe. "Where did he go?"

"Maybe back to the Visitor Center. Kathy's SUV is still in the parking lot."

"You think she did it?"

"I think we can sure as hell ask her. Whoever it was knew the lay of the land."

"If Kathy drinks even half of what it appears she does, I don't see how she could hold a gun steady. "

Cade nodded. "I don't know. She and her husband used to shoot skeet at a club in Memphis. I don't know if they still do." He crouched down and examined the ground. "It's too dry and grassy to tell for sure, but someone certainly could have stood here. Maybe Ralph. This is his land and his project."

"You think he'd try to shoot me?"

"Maybe *he* killed Wendell. Maybe that's what Debra wanted to tell you."

"Maybe," she said doubtfully. "But we have a long list of suspects and absolutely no proof."

"That's right." He met her gaze, fire blazing from his blue eyes. "And for that reason, from now on you do as I say."

For an instant his fury took her aback. "Excuse me?" she snapped. Was he that concerned about her safety? Or just that determined to stay in control of the investigation?

She couldn't let him bully her. They were equally responsible for this case, and she had to prove that she was his equal in everything. She wasn't jockeying with him for control, but he did have a disturbing tendency toward protectiveness.

But was she interpreting him correctly? Did he feel protective toward her, and want to keep her safe? Or did he just doubt her ability?

After a searching gaze that almost dissolved her indignation, he turned his attention to the area below. After a final sweep of the area, he holstered his weapon.

"You would never order Fred or Shelton around like that."

He turned those fiery eyes on her again. "They're not as stubborn as you are."

"Stubborn? You listen to me, Dupree. I'm an FBI special agent *and* a criminologist. This is my purview. And we're equals on this case. Remember, *you* requested the FBI's assistance."

"*Assistance* being the operative word." His glare softened. "You aren't hurt, are you?"

"No. But I appreciate you asking. Finally."

"Well, it's obvious the bullet missed you."

The bullet. She stared at him for a second. "The bullet—I've got to—" She turned and ran.

"What the hell—"

She heard him, but she didn't stop. She had to find those bullets, because she had a sinking feeling that she knew whose gun the bullets came from.

About halfway down, Cade caught up to her and

grabbed her arm. She wrenched it away and nearly tripped over a branch.

"What's wrong?"

"The bullets—" She gasped. "I've got to find them."

"Damn, Gillespie. They're not going anywhere."

He stopped her again in front of the crime-scene tape.

"Cade, let me go in first," she said. "I need to bag that piece of false nail I found. I was just about to do that when—"

He lifted his hands, palms up. "Go ahead."

Cade watched Laurel slip under the tape and step carefully over to the place where Debra's body had lain. She planted her feet in the indentations where she'd stood before, then crouched down. She picked up something off the ground. It looked like a miniature ballpoint pen. She used it to lift a leaf.

He heard a satisfied sound from her. "Here it is."

Her hand didn't even shake. He was amazed at how calm she was after almost being shot. He kept waiting for reaction to set in. But right now she was all confidence and efficiency as she scraped the pink nail fragments into a plastic evidence bag with the point of the pen, then sealed it.

Straightening, she held the bag out to him.

He snagged it in his fingers and pocketed it.

Meanwhile, she turned and gazed up at the rise from which the shot had come. She frowned and shifted a few millimeters to her right, glanced at the trunk of the tree, then back toward the rise.

With a start, he realized what she was doing. She was reliving the moment when the gun went off. Based on her level of concentration, he figured she was judging what she'd heard and how far away it had been from her ear. A chill slithered down his spine.

After another few seconds of quiet study, she pointed her finger toward the rise, then swept it past her temple.

Alarm ripped through him like a laser as the tip of her finger scooped the air less than three inches from her cheekbone.

The bullet's path. The shooter was either damn good or damn lucky. The bullet had traveled over a hundred feet and still barely missed her.

Laurel dug into her jeans again, this time the front pocket. She pulled out a knife. Opening it, she burrowed into the tree trunk.

"That's a long way for a bullet from a handgun to travel. They were nearly spent when they hit. Probably wouldn't have killed me," she commented casually.

"Probably?" Cade felt sweat prickling his neck and back. He couldn't stop a grisly vision of the bullet impacting the side of her head.

After a few seconds, she retrieved another bag from her pocket. Turning it inside out, she inserted her fingertips into it and extracted the bullet from the tree trunk. Holding it with the plastic bag, she examined it closely.

"Just as I thought," she muttered as she turned the bag right side out around the bullet and sealed it.

Stuffing it into her pocket, she went to work on the second bullet.

"Leave it. We can dig it out later, after I get a picture of it. Right now I want to talk to Kathy before she leaves the Visitor Center."

She looked at the tree, then back at him.

"That bullet came from my gun," she said.

He'd half-suspected that. What he didn't know was how she could be so certain. "How can you know it's your gun?"

Her lips turned up. "Ancient FBI trick." She held out the bag. "Jack O'Hara, one of my colleagues in the Unsolved Mysteries Division, taught me years ago to mark my cartridges. See right there on the side? That's an L. Whoever stole my gun killed Debra, and probably Wendell."

"And now he's trying to kill you," Cade said.

Chapter Nine

"Of course I didn't shoot at anyone. What kind of question is that?" Kathy set her cigarette on the edge of the counter near the sink in the kitchen area of the Visitor Center.

"Kathy, hold it—" Laurel started, but Kathy plunged her hands into a sinkful of soapy water. Too late. "We need to swab your hands for GSR."

"For what?" Kathy didn't look up. She fished out a washcloth and picked up a large platter.

"Gun shot residue. Take your hands out of the water please."

"I told you I didn't shoot at anyone."

Cade stepped up beside Kathy and took hold of her wrists. He gently lifted them out of the water.

"Hey!"

"Just trying to help," he said.

Kathy slung water and suds off her hands. "You'd better watch out, Cade Dupree. I'll charge you with police brutality."

He ignored her. "Laurel, swab her fingers. Maybe we can still get something."

"There's nothing to get, Cade. Do I need to call Harrison?" Kathy asked.

"Do you need a lawyer?" he responded.

Laurel set the crime-scene kit they'd brought in with them on the counter. Cigarette smoke burned her eyes. She picked up the forgotten cigarette and doused it in the water and then tossed it into the trash.

Quickly, she prepared a swab and ran it over Kathy's soapy hands. Why would Kathy, who'd probably never washed a dish without gloves on, be so eager to immerse her hands in suds moments after a gun was fired not thirty yards away?

Because she was the shooter?

"Where did Langston go?" Cade asked.

"How should I know? He drove off, still cursing you for messing up his construction schedule."

Laurel pressed her lips together. It was all she could do to hold her temper in the face of Kathy's disdain. "What about you? What have you been doing?"

Kathy's glare could have withered a tree. She turned to Cade. "Cade, what is going on here?"

"Someone fired a handgun from over the rise a few minutes ago. Nearly hit Laurel."

Kathy's eyes widened. "That's awful. No wonder you're concerned. I didn't hear a thing." She spread her fingers. "Do you need to do another swab?"

"No. You're fine," Laurel said shortly. "But we would like to check your purse and your vehicle."

Kathy waved a hand, sending soap bubbles flying. "Of course. I have nothing to hide. One condition, though." Her attention was still on Cade. "You have to promise me you won't charge me if you find an open bottle."

"Kathy—"

"Come on, Cade. I'm just kidding. I don't *think* there's a bottle in there."

Cade glanced at Laurel. She shook her head. She didn't

want to leave Kathy alone for an instant. "You go ahead and check her car," she said. "I'll go through her purse."

He nodded. "Be right back."

"Where's your purse?" Laurel asked Kathy.

"Right over there. Can I dry my hands now?"

Laurel glanced at the stack of dishes on the counter. "Aren't you going to finish washing those dishes?"

Kathy cut her with a look. "No. I'm late for an appointment." Her hands still trembled and she looked slightly green around the gills.

Laurel headed for the table. She carefully emptied the contents of a designer bag that had probably cost more than an FBI agent's salary for two months onto the table. There were the usual things—wallet, lipstick, compact, various crumpled receipts and folded money, a package of tissues, a glasses case and a small flask that was at least three-quarters full.

When Laurel set down the flask she noticed an oily residue on her hands. She sniffed her fingers then sniffed the smooth surface of the flask. It was gun oil—a specific brand that smelled like bananas. She glanced at Kathy who was having trouble lighting her cigarette.

She picked up the flask by its top. "We're going to need to take this with us."

Kathy's eyes narrowed as the cigarette finally caught and silver smoke curled around her face. She drew in a lungful. "What for?"

"We're checking for fingerprints—mostly for elimination purposes."

Laurel pulled an exam glove onto her right hand, and then placed the flask into an evidence bag. As she was sealing it Cade came back in holding a half-empty bottle of liquor.

"I'm taking this with me," he said to Kathy. "I've called

Officer Phillips to come and take you home to change clothes. We're going to need your shoes and dress. I believe they're the same ones you were wearing last night?"

"It's not nice to notice something like that, Cade."

"I apologize."

The door opened again and Shelton Phillips walked in. "Morning, Mrs. Adler. Special Agent Gillespie."

"Hi," Laurel said.

Kathy nodded.

"You ready to go, Mrs. Adler?"

"Shelton, when you get the dress and shoes, take them and Mrs. Adler to the station. Take her statement about her movements last night and then drive her back here to pick up her vehicle," Cade said.

"Yes, sir."

"You ready?" he asked Laurel.

Laurel nodded in relief. She was more than ready for this day to end. She was tired, and reaction to her near miss was setting in.

In the pickup, she held up the evidence bag. "I found an oily residue on this flask from Kathy's purse. It's a type of gun oil that smells like bananas." She held the bag close to his nose.

"Hard to mistake that smell. What do you think she was doing to get gun oil on a whisky flask?"

"Cleaning a gun and drinking? Shooting a gun and drinking? But most likely, she carried a gun in her purse and some oil got on the flask."

"What about the rest of the contents of the purse?"

"I didn't mention the gun oil to her—I didn't want to make a big deal out of it, so I took the flask instead of the whole bag. Let her assume it was because she was carrying booze."

"So what do you think?"

"I think she's the one who shot at me." Laurel cringed at the idea of Kathy's trembling fingers aiming the gun. "I want to swab the flask and send it with the rest of the evidence. Then we'll have verification. And if she fired it then put it in her purse, GSR may have rubbed off on the flask. I doubt we're going to get any off her hands."

"That means we can't charge her." He paused. "Was it your gun?"

"I don't use that brand of oil. Can't stand the smell. But I suppose she could have cleaned the gun. My question is, can she possibly be that good a shot?"

He shook his head as he pulled up in front of the police station.

"Cade, do you think Kathy killed Debra?"

"I don't know, but it's beginning to look like she was trying to kill you."

LAUREL STOOD in Cade's office a couple of hours later, looking down at the meager evidence they'd gathered. Lined up on his desk were the plastic bags that held the graduation night pictures, Debra's broken false nail, the crime-scene photos, the French nail from Laurel's room at the B&B, the bullet and Kathy's flask.

She stared at the slug she'd dug out of the tree, the slug that had missed her skull by less than three inches. At the time, she'd managed to hold herself together. She'd been all business—all FBI, estimating trajectory, pinpointing where the shooter must have stood, preserving the evidence.

But now, in the safety of the police station, staring at the misshapen piece of lead, it was all she could do to hold herself together. Her stomach felt like it had been turned upside down—or inside out. Her head spun with the realization of how close she'd come to death.

She was a criminologist, but most of the time she never saw the crime scene. Working for the Division of Unsolved Mysteries, her participation usually consisted of going over old case files, re-examining evidence and occasionally disinterring a body for a forensic autopsy.

Until she'd come back to Dusty Springs, the only time she'd actually drawn her weapon or processed a crime scene was during training.

And she'd *never* been shot at—not with real bullets.

Cade's office chair screeched as he leaned back and propped his boots on the desktop. The chair's unoiled springs protested again when he pushed it to a slightly greater angle. He balanced the phone's handset between his ear and shoulder.

"Cade Dupree here, chief of police in Dusty Springs. I need to speak to the medical examiner."

He waved Laurel toward a scarred desk and an ancient chair on the other side of the room, but she shook her head.

She couldn't sit right now. She was too antsy. She reached out and touched the bag that held the bullet. The bag was crooked, just slightly out of alignment with the other six bags. As she adjusted it, her fingers trembled. She pulled her hand back and plunged both fists into the pockets of her jeans.

Stepping over to the cork bulletin board, she pretended to read the notices stuck up there with various thumbtacks, pushpins and a few straight pins. But the bullet lying on the desk behind her taunted her with its nauseating truth— she'd almost died out there today.

She was as spooked as a civilian—more. She'd watched interviews with victims of near-fatal shootings who were much calmer than she felt right now.

Laurel's brain was whirling. She was wound as tight as the spring on Cade's chair. Wound so tight she wanted to scream. She wished for something—anything—to stop the memory that ran in an endless loop in her head. The replay of that split-second when the slug had whizzed by her head and thunked into the tree trunk.

A metallic shriek and a thud made her jump. A moment later she realized the noise was Cade sitting up and planting his boots on the floor.

She turned in time to catch him frowning as he picked up a pencil and pushed a stack of paper aside. He was still on his phone. "Key? Okay. In her left pocket." He jotted something on the desk blotter. "Wrapped in a tissue?"

Key. Debra had had a key in her pocket? Laurel met his gaze and he moved his head a few millimeters in a nod.

She knew he was thinking the same thing she was. Debra may have been bringing that key to Laurel as evidence. If it fit Laurel's room at the B&B, it would explain how the intruder got in.

"We need that key. Can you send it over by courier? Yeah, the fibers, too. I'm pretty crippled here. I only have two officers and one is the victim's father." He set the pencil down and rubbed his eyes. "How soon can you get it here? Great. Thanks." He hung up.

Laurel barely waited until the phone hit the cradle. "Debra was bringing me a key wrapped in a tissue. It had to be to my room. And it's got prints on it, I'm sure! She knew who ransacked my room. Maybe she did it."

Cade sent her a cautious look. "We'll have to wait and see."

"Wait? We don't have time to wait. We need information. What did the ME say about the cause of death?" Laurel planted her palms on the desk. "The autopsy report? Is he sending us photos? I need to see the marks on her neck—get a closer look at the bruising."

"Settle down. You're about five seconds from a

meltdown. Let me take you to the house so you can relax—maybe take a hot shower."

She shook her head. "No. Stop treating me like a girl. I'm a cop, just like you are. So when *you* stop to take a hot shower, I'll join you."

Cade's eyebrows shot up.

"What?" she snapped.

His cheeks turned faintly pink and he shook his head. "Nothing."

"What other physical evidence did he find? You mentioned fibers. Were they her fingernails? I've got to look at everything before I can make a determination—"

"Hold it." Cade held up his hands. "We do know about procedure down here in Dusty Springs. The ME is faxing me his autopsy report and emailing me hi-res images of his autopsy photos. We'll get a look at them in a few minutes."

"Good. Fine." She slid her hands out of her pockets and rubbed her temples as she paced back and forth across the small office. She twisted her hair up off her neck, but as usual, she didn't have a barrette or a clip to hold it so she let it drop back to swinging just above her shoulders. Then she looked at her watch, still pacing.

"How long will it take the courier to get here? I want to overnight all the evidence to the FBI lab. They can lift a print off almost anything." She reached the front of the room and whirled on her heel and retraced her steps.

"If we call early enough," she continued, "we can get it picked up this evening. Mitch will have the lab in D.C. process it priority and get us some preliminary results by Tuesday at the latest."

At the opposite end of the room, she turned again. This time she ran slap into Cade's hard, warm body. How had he gotten up without the chair squeaking?

"I said hold on." He put his hands on her upper arms and squeezed. "Settle down. We'll get it all done. You need to chill." He ducked his head a little to meet her gaze.

"Chill? You think I should *chill* while there's a killer out there?" She shook her head and tried to extricate herself from his grip. "There's no way. I already let Misty get hurt, and now Debra's dead."

She looked at his big, long-fingered hands, dark against the paler skin of her arms. "Let go of me. I need to move."

He held on. "Yeah, so I see. Why is that?"

She pulled against his grasp.

"That wasn't a rhetorical question. You're nervous as a cat. It's wearing you out."

"It helps me think." She rubbed her temples. "Usually. But right now all I can think about is Debra out there waiting for me, not knowing she was about to die."

"Are you telling me you feel responsible for Debra's death?"

As hard as she tried, she couldn't stop the lump that was growing in her throat. She swallowed and blinked, and tried again to escape Cade's hold.

"I didn't take her seriously," she said, not looking at him. "I should have insisted that she meet me right then, when she called. And then I wasted time dancing with you when I should have been with her—"

"Okay, stop. It's not your fault that Debra was killed. All you did was agree to meet with her. If she told someone what she was doing, or if someone saw her, that's not your responsibility." He stared into her eyes. "Got it?"

His blue gaze was reassuring, but her guilt wasn't that easily assuaged. She'd been lusting after Cade while Debra was dying.

"I tell you what. Why don't I make you some coffee?

You can lie down on the couch in the other room for a while, just until the courier gets here with the key."

"Coffee? Lie down? I can't do that." She wrenched away from him. "Would you stop treating me like—"

Cade's smile faded and his gaze froze her in place. "Like a girl? That's not going to be easy."

Laurel's cheeks flamed. "I don't see why not."

"Then you don't see what I see."

What did he see? She wanted so badly to ask him, but what if all he meant was that he couldn't avoid seeing what any man saw—boobs, lips…boobs? That would be unbearable.

If he really was looking, she wanted him to see *her.* Who she was inside. Who she'd always been, even behind the teenaged awkwardness, the braces and glasses. For what little good it would do her.

Even if he did think of her as more than a fellow law enforcement officer, even if his casual flirtations were partly genuine, it wouldn't matter. She'd never been good at the flirtatious banter that went on between men and women. She had an annoying habit of speaking her mind, when she wasn't too flustered to speak at all. She'd missed out on a lot of dates because she'd never learned how to flirt.

"Hey." He touched her chin with his fingertip, gently urging her to look at him. "Surely you look in the mirror."

She shrugged, caught by his gaze again. This time his blue eyes were smoky and soft. His scent filled her head— fresh, woodsy, unbearably sexy.

His finger slid along her chin to her jawline. "What do you see when you look in the mirror?"

Another opportunity for a cute, flip remark. But her mind was blank. All she could think of was the truth. "Red hair, freckles. A too-big mouth and a too-short nose."

"Man. You're really fishing for compliments, aren't you?"

"Fishing? No, of course not."

His gaze roamed over her face. "You're not, are you? You don't know you're a knockout, Gillespie?"

Her face burned. "I'll bet you say that to all the FBI agents."

His killer grin appeared. "Look, ladies and gentlemen. She *can* flirt."

She laughed and stepped backward, putting distance between herself and him, distance that would hopefully dissipate the intense sensation that was surging through her—a sensation she could only name as lust.

"Good job distracting me, Dupree," she said, trying to keep her voice casual. "I'm fine now. Thanks."

His expression softened and he took a step toward her. "It's a tough job, but somebody's got to do it. I'm available any time you need distracting."

Don't kiss me. As soon as the thought formed in her head, she had to suppress a laugh at herself. He wasn't going to kiss her. All he was doing was a little harmless flirting to take her mind off her brush with death and the weight of her responsibility for Debra.

But he dipped his head a little more and laid a hand on her shoulder. "I'm sorry I wasn't there."

Oh, don't. Don't be unbearably sweet and protective. "Nothing to be sorry for. Getting shot at is part of the job."

"But it's never happened to you before, has it?"

"Yes. Well, no." A shudder racked her body. "Not with real bullets."

He laughed softly. "Just at Quantico."

She nodded miserably. "I can't believe I'm so shook up over one shot."

"Two shots. And you ought to be. I am."

"You? Why?" She raised her gaze to his and saw the tenderness she'd dreaded.

Cade shook his head in wonder. "You have to ask?" His fingers touched her cheek. With the slightest pressure, he urged her head up. "I'd never forgive myself if something happened to you."

His voice was low and gentle, surrounding her with the promise of safety. It was also rough and sexy, rumbling through her, sending deep tremors of awareness straight to her core. She couldn't draw breath to speak as he caressed the underside of her chin, the sensitive line of her jaw. She couldn't breathe when he moved his hand over the nape of her neck to curve protectively around the back of her head.

"Um, have *you* ever been shot?"

He chuckled and his breath fanned across her mouth. "Only once. By Old Man Rabb."

His thumb caressed the soft skin beneath her ear.

She could barely think. "The guy who shot his son-in-law in the butt?"

"The very same."

"Wh-where did he shoot you?"

His eyes twinkled. "In his front yard."

"I meant—"

He bent his head and lowered his gaze to her mouth. "I know what you meant," he whispered.

Then he kissed her.

At first it was nothing more than a brush of sensation across her lips, like the flutter of a butterfly's wing. His fingers tightened when she let her lips part. He kissed her more deeply, using his tongue to taste her, to trace her lips and invade their boundaries.

She heard a plaintive moan, and realized it had come from her own throat. Cade reacted with a sharp intake of breath. He widened his stance and wrapped his arm around her waist, then pulled her close.

Laurel felt his need through the double barrier of their jeans. Her breasts tightened. Her nipples scraped against the soft cotton of her T-shirt.

All her carefully honed defenses melted at the feel of him—hot and hard, pressing against her.

He wanted her. The thought empowered her. This was Cade Dupree, her first major crush. Back in high school he hadn't known she existed. Well, he knew now. She felt his knowledge in his hard, insistent arousal.

She kissed him back with rising passion. Her knees wobbled and her insides turned to liquid heat. If he weren't holding her up, she'd crumple at his feet.

He pushed her two steps backward. Her back hit the wall and at the same time, Cade freed his hands and slipped them under her shirt. He caressed the bare skin of her belly and back.

The almost-aggressive gesture flooded her with hot longing. He was dominating her, holding her immobile, as his desire for her became more and more insistent.

She flattened her palms against his chest, not to push him away, but to soak up the surge of life within him. His breath came hard and steady. She lifted her head to look at him and he kissed the tip of her nose.

Laurel's thoughts were as jumbled as her emotions. Her desire was as all encompassing as his arms. She struggled to clear her muddled brain, but he was nibbling on her ear. Heaven help her she was about to come just from the feel of his mouth on her.

She tried to concentrate on their reason for being here, but he was doing things to her insides like nothing she'd ever experienced.

He propped a forearm on the wall above her head and leaned in toward her, letting his chest skim the sensitized tips of her breasts just like his lips were skimming the ultra-sensitive spot beneath her ear. Desire flowed through her like hot lava, wiping all thoughts from her head.

Her body went boneless as he pressed closer. She spread her fingers on his chest and encountered his nipples. A quiet hiss in her ear told her she'd discovered an erogenous zone, maybe one no one had explored before. A thrill of power sent her desire climbing higher.

What would she give to show Cade Dupree something he'd never experienced?

She curled her fingers, grasping handfuls of his shirt, as she sought his mouth. He brought his attention from her earlobe and jaw back to her lips and kissed her more deeply than he had yet. Her bones melted as desire pooled between her thighs.

A knock on the door sent them hurtling away from each other.

Cade wiped a hand across his mouth and grimaced at the ache in his loins. As he forced himself back from the brink of full arousal, the knob turned.

He worked to compose his face. What the hell was he thinking? He'd lost all sense of time and space for a few seconds.

He clamped down on his tongue, using the shock of pain to deflate his arousal. He tasted blood. Even so, his effort wasn't entirely successful.

"Probably the courier," he muttered, turning his back on Laurel and heading behind his desk.

The door slammed open and Ralph Langston stomped in. His gaze flickered over Cade's face, then stopped short when he saw Laurel. His dark eyes bounced back and forth between them.

Cade risked a glance at her flaming cheeks and too-bright eyes. She finger-combed her hair and tried to look nonchalant. She didn't succeed. In fact she looked about as far from nonchalant as a woman could. She looked flushed and supple and turned on.

Langston's eyes twinkled. "Sorry to bother you, Dupree. I see you were interrogating Laurel."

Jerk! Cade ground his knuckles into his palm, quelling the urge to deck the man. "I hope you're here to solidify your alibi for last night," he growled.

"My alibi? What are you talking about?"

"According to what you told Special Agent Gillespie, you were in the main room of the Visitor Center all night. But you won't name anyone who can corroborate that. You want to think about your answer?"

"I don't have to think about it. Am I the only attendee at that party whose whereabouts can't be verified?"

"That's not the point. The point is, you don't ever seem to have a witness to your activities. How do you explain that?"

"Once again, Chief, you're asking me to prove a negative. I was in plain sight in the Visitor Center the whole evening. If you can't unearth a witness that will tell you that, it's not my problem."

"What did you come here for?" Cade snapped.

"I want that crime-scene tape taken down. I'm paying through the nose for that equipment, and I want to get the land down by the creek bank cleared *today*."

"Not going to happen."

"You can't do this. It's my land. I paid good money for it."

Good money? That was a matter of dispute. Cade shook

his head and sat behind his desk. "It's my crime scene until I say otherwise."

Langston's gaze dropped to the row of plastic bags on the edge of the desk. Cade had to resist the urge to sweep them across the desk and into a drawer. How much could Langston see? Could he read Cade's bold writing across the face of each bag?

"You crawled all over the area last night," Langston said. "What else do you expect to find down there?" He took a step forward.

Cade pushed his chair back and came around the desk, casually propping a hip on the corner so that his thigh blocked Langston's view of the evidence.

Langston's eyes narrowed and his face flushed. He backed up a step and shifted his gaze toward the back of the office.

"Why don't you tell me what I can expect to find?" Cade asked, crossing his arms. He'd like nothing more than to throw Langston out of his office, but he needed to hear what the man had to say. "You and Kathy Adler were tromping all over the scene this morning. Were you two just out for a stroll?"

"Kathy wanted to see if she could find anything that would help catch whoever killed Debra."

Right. Cade exchanged a glance with Laurel and knew she was thinking the same thing he was. Kathy Adler had never thought about anyone but herself in her life.

"And you?"

Langston pulled his attention away from the back door of the office. He showed his amazingly straight, unnaturally white teeth. "Just helping out a friend."

"Fine. Help me out and stay away from my crime scene."

"Don't forget that *your* crime scene is on my land."

"Trust me. I haven't forgotten that. In fact I find it very interesting."

Langston took another step forward. This time his full attention was on Cade. "Now what are you implying?"

"I'm not *implying* anything. I'm telling you straight out, don't mess with my crime scene. If you do I'll arrest you for obstruction of justice."

"I'm talking to my lawyer."

Cade shrugged. "Whatever you need to do. Just don't leave town without asking."

Langston whirled on his handmade Italian leather heel and stomped out of the office.

Cade turned his attention to Laurel for the first time since Langston had walked in. He felt a keen disappointment that her face was no longer flushed, her body no longer supple and open and her eyes had lost the dewy sparkle of sexual hunger.

His loins tightened at the memory of how turned on she'd been. But the sore place on his tongue reminded him of just how close he'd been to losing control.

He had no business thinking about sex right now. He had a murderer to catch. A cop could get in big trouble if he let his libido do the thinking.

"What do you think that was about?" he asked her, forcing his brain to evaluate Langston's actions.

Laurel tugged on the tail of her short orange T-shirt. "He didn't come here to complain about his construction timeline."

He nodded as he straightened. "Right. Did you see what he was trying to do?"

She nodded. "He couldn't take his eyes off the evidence bags until you blocked his view with your—" her gaze drifted down his torso for an instant "—self."

She looked so miserable that he felt sorry for her, even

as he clamped his jaw to keep from smiling at how hard she was working not to look at his thighs.

She walked over to where Langston had stood, then glanced back at her previous position. Her gaze sharpened and her eyebrows rose. "He also checked out the layout of the office." She took a half step to her left. "Is that the evidence room at the end of the hall?"

"Yeah." He straightened and stepped over beside her. "That's what he was looking at?"

"He wasn't looking at me."

"So he came here to see what evidence we have. Think he's planning a break-in?"

"I don't think he likes getting his hands dirty. After all, he has to preserve those buffed nails. On the other hand—" she straightened "—I think he'd dig six feet down in dirt with his bare hands if that's what it took to get what he wanted. Which is exactly why I want to get this stuff packed off to D.C. as soon as possible."

"I agree. But there's no reason we both have to wait here. I'll take you to the house so you can relax. Then once the courier gets here, I'll call FedEx and get it all shipped to D.C. tonight."

"Why are you so anxious to get rid of me all of a sudden?"

"I'm not. But look at you. You're a wreck."

"Thank you so much."

"You were shot at. You're pale as a ghost and you haven't eaten all day. We'll stop and get you a burger. Then you can take a nap. I need to go over Wen—" He stopped and an almost imperceptible grimace crossed his face. "I need to do some paperwork."

Laurel's gaze snapped to his. "You don't want me to see Wendell Vance's case file. That's why you're trying to get rid of me. Well, I'm not leaving. I have to see it."

"No, you don't. You'll be a lot more help to me if you'd just do what I say."

She stuck out her chin. "You mean do what I'm told and stay out of your hair?" Her eyes flashed green and gold. "Maybe I will. I'll just go and leave you to study Wendell's case file."

Her expression had turned positively angelic. Cade eyed her suspiciously. "You're not just going away. I'm taking you back to my house and locking you in."

"Lock me in? Not a chance, Dupree. In fact, I think I'll run back over to the crime scene. I'd like to search around the Swinging Oak—see if I can find any pieces of the chain from the missing medal."

Cade threw up his hands and bit off a very rude curse. "The hell you will. Okay fine. I'll bring Wendell's file home with me. We can review it together."

"Good. I'm glad you finally see it my way."

He shook his head. "Trust me, Gillespie. I do *not* see it your way. That's not why I'm doing this."

Her angelic expression turned more beatific. "It's not? Then why are you?"

"Because I can't trust you as far as I can throw you. Maybe it doesn't mean much to you that someone's obviously trying to harm you, but it does to me."

That stopped her. Her eyes widened. "It does?"

"Yeah." That wasn't what he'd meant. Okay, it was what he'd meant but it wasn't what he'd meant to *say*. Feeling flayed open by his unintentional revelation, he scrambled to think of a flip answer.

"Yeah. Because if anyone around here is going to shoot or strangle you, it's going to be me."

Chapter Ten

A couple of hours later, Cade was sitting at his living room table with an open pizza box and a large manila envelope next to him. He looked up, took in Laurel's T-shirt and pajama pants, then went back to flipping through loose pages.

"Wendell's case file?" she asked. She took a handful of paper napkins and eagerly helped herself to a good-size slice of pizza.

Cade nodded, chewing.

"Did you get the evidence sent?"

He nodded. "I told you I would. They picked it up about eight, just before I came home. The ME sent a sample of Debra's DNA with the key. And yes, he sent the fibers."

"What color were they?"

"They looked black or maybe dark gray."

"Great. That eliminates no one. Over half the people at the party had on black—including me."

"We'll get specifics. We can match the fibers to the clothing Shelton collected."

"I just hope we got them all. Did he get Kathy's dress?"

He nodded.

"So everything is on its way. Hopefully the lab can identify the fibers. If they're unusual at all maybe we can trace them to the piece of clothing they came from. I'm praying they can lift DNA from that false nail. But even so, you never know where you're going to fall in the testing schedule. DNA results can come back in a few days or not for six months. Did FedEx say they'd get it there early?" Laurel asked.

"Before nine."

"Great. Mitch will have some preliminary findings for us by tomorrow afternoon. By then I want to be through reviewing Wendell's file. It's possible that our evidence will lead us to something that your dad missed the first time around."

Cade didn't say anything. She knew he was sensitive about his dad. "You feel responsible for your dad's stroke, don't you?"

His face turned dark as a storm cloud. "Hell, no, I don't. That was James's fault. He went and got himself killed. He was always taking risks. Always thinking he was some kind of superhero. He *knew* he was Dad's—" Cade tossed down a crust of pizza and picked up a fresh slice.

"Screw it," he muttered, then took a big bite.

Laurel saw the same expression on his face that she'd seen at his dad's house. Love, of course, and a slightly impatient indulgence of his dad's infirmities. But there had been something else—a wistfulness. At the time she'd figured it was a wish to have back the strong, competent father he'd known all his life.

But now, behind the vehemence of his anger at his brother, behind the denial that he felt responsible for what James's death had done to his father, she still heard that note. And before he'd bitten off his words, she knew what he'd been about to say.

Dad's *favorite*. The unspoken word made her want to

cry. Cade had given up his own dream to come home and be the dutiful son, because the son his father had always wanted was dead.

"Cade, I'm sorry about your brother—and your dad."

"Yeah, well, that's not your responsibility." He flipped through a few pages.

"Here. Here's where Dad described seeing Wendell for the first time. *Bishop Carter discovered the body of Wendell Vance around 5:00 a.m. on the morning of Sunday, June 21, the day after Vance's high-school graduation. Carter stated he did not touch the body. When I arrived on the scene, Vance was hanging from the Swinging Oak by the rope swing. The rope was knotted around his neck, and a few links of chain were caught between the rope and Wendell's neck. (See evidence bag marked #1.)*"

Cade looked up. "Just like Dad said."

Laurel nodded. "Where are the evidence bags? Is that them?" She reached for a padded folder Cade had lain aside. "Do you mind if I look?"

He shook his head. "Careful, though. If there's anything in there that's not—"

"Bagged. I know. I'll be careful." She opened the envelope and cautiously emptied the contents onto the tabletop.

"Not much."

"There's the chain."

She nodded. "And the rope. And a few pictures. Look."

She studied an instant camera snapshot of Wendell hanging from the Swinging Oak. Wendell's face looked peaceful, and it wasn't discolored.

Another photo recorded the ground below his feet. The area was muddy, with water standing in the furrows made by footprints. A third was a close-up of his face after he'd been cut down.

"All that water. Your dad didn't have an easy time with that crime scene."

Cade flipped another page. "He's got a note here saying the ground right there stays wet during most of the summer."

Laurel jumped up, retrieved a lighted magnifying glass from her overnight bag and brought it back to the table. She studied the close-up of Wendell's face and neck.

"What are you looking for?" Cade asked.

"Trying to get a sense of how he died. I see the bruising from the broken hyoid bone. I see marks made by the rope. What I don't see is the lividity consistent with death by hanging."

"Dad told me a crushed hyoid bone could cause death instantly."

"He's right. And that could be what happened. Does he say if he got any fingerprints?"

Cade latched on to another slice of pizza while he searched through the file. "Nope. Here are some notes. Looks like the rope was too rough, the piece of chain was badly smudged and Wendell's skin didn't show anything. Dad says he couldn't lift a print."

"We could send the chain to the FBI lab. Technology has changed a lot in the past ten years." She picked up the photo, holding it so it caught the light and moved the magnifying glass closer. "Wait a minute. It's hard to tell, but I think there might be two different sets of bruises on his neck."

"Two sets? Show me."

She held out the picture and the glass. Cade wiped his fingers on a napkin, then took the magnifying glass.

"I don't see it. Maybe you're seeing shadows."

"Maybe, but this picture definitely goes to the lab. What if somebody choked him and then hanged him?"

She took a long drink of cola, then looked at the can. "Oh, man, I probably won't sleep a wink tonight."

Cade looked up and she had to ignore the heat in his gaze that suggested being awake all night for certain reasons might not be a bad thing.

She nodded at her drink. "Caffeine."

He straightened and rubbed his eyes. "So stop drinking cola and turn in. It's after twelve. If Decker sends us any of that evidence tomorrow we're going to be busy."

She yawned. "Not a bad idea. Are you ready for bed?"

His hot blue gaze ignited flames of awareness when he centered it on her breasts. How could he make her react just by looking at her? As if taunting her for even asking, her breasts tightened and she sucked in a sharp little breath.

Embarrassed, she jumped up. The sheet and blanket she'd used the night before were folded on the end of the couch, just like she'd left them. She picked up the sheet, but by the time she got it unfolded, Cade was by her side, reaching for it.

"I've got it," she said.

"I'll help you make up the couch."

"No. I've got it." He was too close, too big and gorgeous and sexy. And she was too near naked, with nothing but a thin layer of cotton covering her.

He reached around her to snag a corner of the sheet, and his forearm brushed her breast.

Electrified pleasure streaked through her. She was horribly afraid she'd gasped aloud again.

He froze, which for her was not a good thing. The tip of her nipple strained toward the slight pressure of his arm, increasing the tingling awareness that branched like lightning through every inch of her.

She heard a quiet, frustrated moan and was chagrined

to realize it had come from her throat. Taking a step backward, her calf hit the edge of the couch and she lost her balance.

Cade caught her before she fell. Now she was stuck in the circle of his long hard arms and in about one second his sexy woodsy scent would hit her and she'd no longer be responsible for what she did.

"Sorry—" she choked out.

"I've got you," he murmured at the same time.

"I don't—"

His hands, warm and rough—a man's hands—wrapped around her upper arms and pulled her to him. "Do you know you're driving me nuts?" he asked gruffly.

She shook her head. "I'm not trying—"

"I know you're not. But could you stop?"

"Stop?" she croaked. She couldn't move, could barely think. All she could do was stare up at him and wait to see what he would do next. Because right now her brain had left the building, and an erotic haze swirled around her, wrapping her in his masculine scent and hard body, so deliciously different from hers.

"Stop being so—aware. Stop looking at me as if you want to crawl into bed with me. Stop being so sexy and irresistible."

Heat suffused her face and prickled her scalp. "Are you accusing me of—of *tempting* you?"

He shook his head and grimaced. "Not on purpose. But you've got to know what you look like in that T-shirt with that wild hair curled around your face."

She'd forgotten to dry and straighten her hair. She must look like a redheaded Medusa.

Cade let go of her arms and stepped backward, glaring at her in exasperation. "I knew it was a bad idea to bring the case file home. I should have stayed at the office. I should have spent the night there." He spiked his fingers through his short hair.

"You *are* blaming me." The heat of embarrassment turned into heat of anger. She poked him in the chest with her forefinger. "Don't you dare—after you forced me to stay here. After you tried to give me your—" she flung her arm out toward his bedroom "—your *bed*."

She stuck her chin out. "I would never look at you like I wanted to crawl into bed with you. How dare you say I look sexy and—and irresistible!"

His brows shot up and that killer smile of his started to grow.

She'd had enough of his accusations and his sexy grin. She was leaving. She stomped off to the bathroom—or she tried to. Her feet tangled in the sheet and she pitched forward.

"Whoa." He lifted her enough to free her feet, then set her down, way too close to him for comfort.

CADE FELT HER RIBS expand under his fingers with each agitated breath. He knew he was acting like an idiot, but that was only because he *was* an idiot.

She was right. He was the one who'd forced her to stay here. He could have gotten her another room at the bed-and-breakfast, or let her stay with his dad.

Dad had a little trouble with certain words but he was otherwise fine. He played golf almost every day and he and Cade had gone to the firing range just a couple of weeks ago. Dad could still shoot a two-inch diameter grouping in the center of the target. Dad would have no trouble defending her.

Meanwhile, as his head swirled with all the things he should have done, Laurel wriggled enticingly. She tried to step around him, but all she managed to do was unbalance them both. They went tumbling onto the couch and he ended up with her sprawled across his chest.

He found himself looking through her tumbled curls straight into her eyes. He'd been fascinated by all the different colors that danced in them from the first time he'd locked gazes with her. Green and gray and brown—shot through with amber and blue and that odd rust color. Surrounded by dark red lashes, they were stunningly beautiful.

And snapping with anger.

He felt her breasts flatten against his chest as she took a breath, but before she could unleash on him he put his palms on either side of her face and kissed her soundly. She gasped against his mouth, but he ignored that and kept on kissing her, nibbling on her lips, waiting to see if she was going to rear back and deck him.

Triumph flared when she relaxed against him. Raging desire engulfed him when she met his exploring tongue with her own. He nearly lost it when she crawled onto his lap. He'd thought he was already hard, but as she maneuvered her butt against his thighs and loins, he grew painfully rigid and pulsed with need.

"This is your fault," she whispered against his mouth. "Not mine."

He pulled back to gauge the expression on her face. Her voice was light and teasing, but her face reflected caution, maybe even apprehension. "I'll take the blame," he panted.

"You ought to be a gentleman and stop us." Her mouth nuzzled his jawline and traced a path to his ear.

"I'm no gentleman." His voice sounded strangled to his own ears as he wrapped his hands around her waist and lifted her so she could straddle him. Then he ran his palms down her hips to her thighs, stroking them gently through the thin cotton pajama pants. He made a heroic effort not to strain toward her in a simulation of lovemaking. He didn't want to scare her.

Her hands were flat against his pecs and her fingers scraped his sensitized nipples. He swallowed hard. She'd done that earlier—and surprised the hell out of him. He'd never noticed how unbearably sensitive they were.

He pushed his fingers into her curls and pulled her head down. This time he didn't stop himself—couldn't. As his mouth closed over hers he thrust rhythmically against her. The hindrance of their clothes made the exquisite torture even more acute.

He wasn't sure how much longer he could last.

Chapter Eleven

Laurel had no idea how she'd gotten to this point. One minute she was preparing to stomp out of Cade's house and the next they were in a heap on his couch. Despite what she'd told him, she was pretty sure that was her fault, not his.

As he kissed her deeply, he rocked against her, driving her toward a sexual mountaintop that she was sure had only one way down. To get there she first had to reach the pinnacle.

"Do you have something?"

"Something?" His fingers crawled up her ribs to the underside of her breasts. Her T-shirt might as well not have been there at all, for all the protection it gave her against his touch. As his thumbs skimmed the tips of her breasts and his hips kept up their erotic rhythm, she felt a deep sense of safety and certainty that she'd never felt before.

"Something," she hissed. "A condom."

His eyes opened, searing blue and heavy-lidded with passion—passion she'd put there. They widened as he assimilated what she'd said.

"I guess so—somewhere."

"You guess so? Don't you—"

His cheeks turned pink and he took a long breath. "Not nearly as much as you might think," he said. He grasped her waist and set her off him. He stood and took her hand, pulling her behind him as he headed for his bedroom.

"Looks like I'm going to get you to crawl into my bed after all."

Laurel let him lead her into his room. She enjoyed the view from behind. His perfect bottom in those gray sweatpants, his back planed with muscle underneath his T-shirt. That enticing curve right above the waistband of his low-slung sweats made her mouth water.

Still, she couldn't let him think he had the upper hand. "Don't push your luck," she rasped.

Just inside his shadowy bedroom, Cade turned and pulled her into his arms. She went willingly despite the little voice in her head telling her what a foolish thing she was doing.

He pulled off his T-shirt. Her hands followed the shirt's tail. His skin was hot and smooth, like thick rich velvet. His flat belly rose and fell with his rapid breathing.

With no thought other than the intense longing to surround herself with him, she pressed her cheek into the hollow of his shoulder.

Breathing deeply of his intoxicating scent, she melted into his arms. Her body curled toward his heat, craving it. He pushed her shirt up, bunching the material across her shoulder blades before tugging it off and letting it fall. His fingers traced the bumps on her spine as he bent his head and kissed her shoulder.

Laurel trembled. She felt like a teenager, like she'd never felt back then. She felt new, beautiful, sexy. He wanted her. Cade Dupree, whom she'd adored with all her teenaged heart, and who had never known she existed, wanted *her*.

With a sigh, he touched her collarbone, then traced a finger down between her breasts. He whispered something, she didn't know what. All her focus was centered on his hands. Then he lifted her and lay her down on his bed.

She watched him push his sweatpants down and off. Her thighs tightened with an almost painful thrill as she saw his naked body for the first time. He was as beautiful as she'd imagined he would be—more than she'd believed any man could be.

He crawled onto the bed next to her, pressed his palm against her belly, then pulled the drawstring on her pajama pants. Sliding his fingers underneath the elastic of her panties, he pushed them down her legs. Slowly he ran his palms up her ankles, her calves, her thighs. Each place he touched burned with the fire of desire.

Stretching out next to her, he kissed her and pressed her close against his body. With his fingers he touched her, opened her, drove her to the edge of climax again and again, only to pull her back and start the journey over.

Finally, desperately, she murmured his name and felt for him. He arched his neck and moaned.

"Sorry," she whispered, jerking her hand away.

But he shook his head. "No," he whispered roughly. "Don't stop. It's good." He took her hand in his, guiding her.

When he raised himself above her, she met his blue gaze and saw the lust and tenderness there. When he gently spread her legs and pushed into her, she cried out with sudden hot pleasure.

"Are you okay?" he whispered hoarsely.

She couldn't speak. Her throat was choked with shock and awe and the promise of tears.

She was no virgin. She'd had a couple of intimate relationships. But nobody had ever measured up to her high-school crush. She'd never realized she'd been comparing them.

He lifted his head, frowning down at her as he touched her damp cheek.

"It's okay. I'm okay," she finally managed to say. For another instant he didn't move, then he kissed her and took her over the edge.

THE SOUND OF his cell phone pulled Cade out of a dreamless sleep. He rolled over to reach for it and encountered firm, supple flesh.

Laurel. His body hardened immediately as he recalled the night and their lovemaking.

Her face was soft and relaxed, her lips parted slightly. That wild hair half covered her face. He touched a curl.

But his phone was still ringing. He had to reach across her to get it. She stirred.

"Dupree," he growled.

"Fire! At the police station."

"Who is this?" But all he heard was a click. *What the hell?* He looked at the display. He knew that number. It was the pay phone on the corner near the station.

He hit his speed dial as he kicked the covers off his legs and stood. But Kit Haydel's cell phone went straight to voice mail. He headed for his dresser and dug out a pair of jeans.

As he tugged them on, his phone rang again. It was Kit.

"Cade. I just got a call about a fire at the police station."

"Yeah, me, too. From the pay phone."

Laurel raised her head. "What is it?"

Cade glanced at her as he reached into his closet. He grabbed the first thing he touched—a white dress shirt. "I'm on my way," he said to Kit.

"I'm rousting the guys."

"Wait. I'll be there in two minutes. It might be a ruse."

"A ruse?"

"Meet me there. Come armed."

As he pocketed his cell phone, Laurel sat up, pulling the sheet up with her. "What is it?"

"Fire. At the station."

"Oh, no." She swung her feet off the bed and looked around for her clothes.

He hopped on one foot then the other, tugging on his running shoes. He knew she wasn't about to let him go alone—not without a fight. But he couldn't figure out which was more dangerous, taking her with him or leaving her here.

Whoever called could be luring them out of the house and into a trap. Or they could be trying to separate them so they could get to Laurel. He wished like hell he knew which.

"You stay here," he barked.

"I'm not staying here while you—"

"Look, Gillespie. I don't have time to argue. This could be a ruse to get us out into the open. The voice was disguised."

She pulled the sheet with her as she retrieved her T-shirt from the floor in front of the bed. "I'm going."

"No!" He rounded on her. "I'm not putting you out there to be shot at again. Get dressed. Get your gun, and stay here."

She opened her mouth but his furious glare must have worked, because she closed it again.

Something in her eyes made him stop for a second. "Stay here," he said softly. "I'll lock the door behind me. Be back in fifteen minutes."

Laurel reached for her T-shirt. She couldn't decide if she was touched by Cade's concern for her safety or furious at him for ordering her around. She had every right to go with him. He'd requested the FBI's help on the case. But a part of her also knew that his reasoning was sound. The killer had already taken a shot at her once.

Her job was to get dressed, get her gun and be ready for anything.

She pulled on jeans and her running shoes.

Thank God they'd overnighted the evidence to D.C. If it was Debra's murderer who had set the fire, he or she was probably hoping to burn up everything connected to the case.

That was definitely encouraging. That meant that the killer knew there was something in the evidence that would lead to him—or her. It also meant they were getting bolder—more desperate. And a desperate criminal was a careless one.

She retrieved her gun from her purse and checked it. She had a full magazine, and a spare that she stuck in her jeans pocket. Then she inserted her paddle holster at the small of her back and seated her weapon in it.

She was ready. She glanced at her watch. Cade had been gone for seven minutes. It seemed like thirty.

She sat down on the couch, where last night she'd lost all reason. Her fingers flew to her mouth. How had she let herself lose control like that? She *never* lost control. But this time it was Cade Dupree.

It was kind of pathetic that she was still totally hung up on her big high-school crush. Way to mature emotionally, Gillespie.

Still, his lovemaking *was* everything she'd imagined it would be, and everything her other relationships had never been. She sighed as an echo of last night's exquisite climax shuddered through her.

At that instant, her cell phone rang. Her heart jumped into her throat.

Cade. She glanced at the clock. Ten minutes. Had something happened? Maybe the fire wasn't just a ruse. Maybe it was real.

But she didn't recognize the number on the phone's

display. What if it was the fire chief? What if something had happened?

"Laurel Gillespie," she answered.

"Are you with Dupree?"

"What? No." Her senses went on alert. "Why?"

"I need your help. I know who killed them."

Laurel gripped the phone more tightly. The voice was muted and obviously disguised. She thought it was a woman but she couldn't be sure. She had to keep them talking.

Apprehension fluttered in the back of her throat but she swallowed against it. "Who is this?" she snapped.

"Please, just listen." The voice rasped harshly in her ears. "I need to talk to you now. It's life or death."

"Okay. Why don't you—"

"Listen to me! There's no time!"

Laurel pressed her lips together. This might be the break they'd been hoping for.

"Meet me at the Swinging Oak. Hurry!"

"*No.* I'm not meeting you anywhere. I'll call Cade—Chief Dupree."

"Fine. Call him. But hurry! They're going to kill me."

"They who?"

"Please, they're coming. For God's sake, help me." The phone went dead.

She stared at the display for a few seconds. She couldn't go out there alone. Cade was almost certainly right. The fire was a ruse to lure her out into the open. She dialed his cell but got no answer.

"Come on. Answer the phone!" She looked at the clock. Seventeen minutes had passed.

"Where are you, Cade?"

Her heart was hammering with apprehension. She'd be an idiot to go out there alone. But if she delayed—Debra's swollen, discolored face rose in her mind. She'd been a few minutes late and Debra had ended up dead.

She couldn't bear another death on her conscience.

She thought about driving by the police station, but that would add another five minutes. Not to mention that Cade wouldn't let her go. She didn't have Officer Phillips's number, so she called Fred. He answered sleepily.

"Fred, it's Laurel. You haven't talked to Cade?" She checked her weapon automatically as she rushed out the door.

"No. What's wrong?"

"I need you to meet me at the Swinging Oak—right now. Can you do that?"

"Sure. What's going on?" His voice was stronger. He was wide awake now.

"I got a call, but it could be a trap."

"Where's Cade?"

"I'll explain. How long will it take you to get there?"

"Five or six minutes."

"Thanks, Fred. Wait for me at the Visitor Center parking lot." As she jumped into her rental car, she heard sirens off in the distance. So the fire was real.

She sped to the Visitor Center and parked right at the edge of the cleared area. Fred's car was already there, he wasn't in it.

Dear heavens, he'd already headed down to the Swinging Oak. Her pulse pounded with apprehension.

She tried Cade's cell phone again. It terrified her that he wasn't answering.

She tried to reassure herself—he'd probably left it in his truck. Still, ominous scenarios swirled through her head. *He was caught in the fire. The killer had ambushed him.*

She shook her head, shaking off the visions, and left him a quick voice message, telling him where she was.

The early morning sunlight reflected off the dew as she walked cautiously into the underbrush using the path that hundreds of kids had walked over the years.

She was worried about Fred, coming down here alone. But she didn't dare call out to him. When she passed the site where Debra had been killed and saw the ends of the torn crime-scene tape fluttering in the slight breeze, guilt stabbed her for more than one reason. Debra had died trying to do the right thing, and Laurel had been too late to save her. And now she'd sent Fred to face the scene of his daughter's murder.

Within twenty paces she was at the edge of the clearing that flanked the bank of the creek. The old Swinging Oak still drooped in the same way it always had. A fragment of the frayed rope that kids had swung on for decades, and which had been used to hang Wendell, hung motionless, unaffected by the hint of an early morning breeze.

Laurel drew her weapon and stepped into the clearing. The first thing she saw was Fred, with a gun to his head. Dread settled like a stone in the pit of her stomach.

"Glad you could make it, Laurel. Drop the gun."

Laurel stared at the woman holding the gun. She looked vaguely familiar. She wasn't a tall woman, but she was muscular, as if she lifted weights. In a sleeveless top and shorts, she was a formidable sight.

"Fred, are you all right?"

"Sorry, Laurel. I should have waited for you." Fred's voice was shaky.

"Look, let me help you," Laurel said to the woman.

But all the woman did was poke the barrel harder into Fred's neck. "Drop the gun or you'll be sorry."

The woman's voice was as shaky and high-pitched with fear as Fred's. Laurel could see the gun barrel quiver against Fred's neck. From her vantage point, she couldn't tell what kind of gun it was, but if it was her stolen Glock, there was no safety on it. In an inexperienced, shaky hand, one wrong twitch or jerk against the trigger and it would all be over.

"Okay. I'm going to put it down," Laurel said quietly. She lowered her gun hand and let her weapon slip to the ground.

"Kick it."

"Look—I can help you—"

"Kick it!"

Laurel pushed the gun with her toe. "Why don't you let Fred go? He's got nothing to do with this. Then you and I can talk."

The woman shook her head. "Don't try to negotiate with me. You're not in charge. I am."

"Okay, but this is between you and me. Not Fred. So why don't you just let him go. He'll leave, won't you, Fred?"

"Shut up!" Sweat beaded on the woman's face. She was terrified of something.

"Why did you bring me here? Obviously nobody's trying to kill you."

"I was supposed to stop you from digging into Wendell's death."

Laurel's stomach turned over. "Stop me? How?"

"I was going to go to Cade's house and confront you after he'd left. But I was afraid he'd come back. He seems a hell of a lot more worried about you than about the police station."

Laurel cursed silently. She'd walked right into this trap. Her fate had been sealed the instant the caller had said her life was in danger.

"You don't want to do anything foolish. I'm betting you've never killed anyone." Laurel was running on pure instinct.

The barrel of the gun pushed harder into Fred's neck and he stiffened. "Don't push me," the woman said.

Laurel cringed at the mounting panic in the woman's voice. She was about to crack. Laurel had to keep her talking, keep her distracted.

"So who's giving you orders to threaten me? Kathy?"

"Oh, please. That lush? I'm just trying to stop you from screwing up everything."

"What everything? Who are you?"

"Shut up!"

"You were there, weren't you? When Wendell was killed. You know what happened." Laurel held her breath. She was bluffing. And she had to win, because if her bluff didn't work, she and Fred could end up dead.

Fred's eyes met hers. He was going to do something.

Fred, no! she wanted to scream, but the other woman was too close to the breaking point. Any sudden move or noise on Laurel's part could get him killed.

"I promise I can help you," she said quietly. "If you'll just—"

"I said shut up. Shut up and listen to me."

Fred doubled his fist and drove his elbow into the woman's gun arm, then whirled, aiming his fist at her jaw.

Her body slammed into a tree and she lost her grip on her weapon. It arced through the air and landed in the brush.

Laurel dove for her own gun. She felt a searing pain along the side of her right foot. Ignoring it, she scooped up the gun just as the woman righted herself and swung a fallen tree branch at Fred's head. He ducked sideways, but the branch caught him on the side of his head. He went limp.

Laurel came up into a crouch, working to get a good grip on her weapon. Before she could get her finger on the trigger, the woman was standing above her. With one swift, spare movement, she kicked the gun out of Laurel's hands.

Laurel's attacker towered over her, bare muscled arms glistening in the sunlight, fists doubled. She looked like she could break Laurel in half without even working up a sweat.

CADE JUMPED OUT of his truck and ran toward the path to the creek bank. He moved as quickly and silently as possible, praying he wasn't too late.

He cursed himself for the hundredth time for not hearing his cell phone. It hardly mattered that the fire truck's sirens had been piercing his eardrums or that the fire's roar had swallowed up all other sound. He should have put the phone on vibrate. He should have heard it.

By the time he realized Laurel had left him a voice mail, fifteen minutes had gone by. Fifteen minutes—plenty of time for her to get herself killed.

The fire had been a distraction to draw him away from her. And it had worked. The inferno started by a potent Molotov cocktail had destroyed the entire front of the station.

As he moved stealthily along the narrow path through the thicket, his decision taunted him. He'd been certain Laurel was safer at his house than out in the open, especially with the chaos of a fire.

He'd been wrong. He'd made the wrong choice and now Laurel was in the clutches of a killer.

Dear God, if she was hurt what would he do? A gnawing pain ate at his heart. If she died—

As he approached the edge of the clearing, he heard a grunt of pain.

He stopped behind a tree and carefully took in the scene before him, his heart hammering in apprehension.

Laurel was on the ground, doubled over in a fetal position.

A woman dressed in a sleeveless tank top and gym shorts, overdeveloped muscles bulging, stood over Laurel with her fists doubled.

As Cade watched, the woman reared back and kicked Laurel in the kidneys. Laurel cried out and scissored her legs, trying to knock the woman's legs out from under her. But her attacker dodged her, bouncing like a boxer.

Then a movement beyond the two of them caught his eye. It was Fred. He was sitting up, one hand to his head where blood flowed freely.

Damn, what had happened here?

Cade drew his weapon. In two strides he had the barrel dug into the side of the woman's neck.

"Don't move," he commanded.

The woman jerked around with amazing strength, but he was ready. He grabbed her arm and wrenched it behind her, never moving his gun barrel from her neck. Then he knocked her feet out from under her and followed her to the ground, his knee in her back.

She grunted and tried to buck him off. She almost succeeded.

He pressed the gun barrel harder into her neck. "Do you not feel this gun?" He dug it a little deeper into her muscled flesh.

She stayed still. He breathed a sigh of relief. *Damn, she was strong.* He hated to admit it but for a second there he hadn't been sure he could wrest that muscle-bound arm behind her.

"Laurel, you okay?" he called without taking his eyes off the woman.

"I—think so."

Her voice was small and quavery. Was she just scared

or was she lying? He wanted to look up, to check for himself, but he didn't dare let down his guard for an instant.

"Fred?"

"I'm okay, Cade. Just a little woozy."

Putting more weight on his knee and not moving the gun a millimeter, Cade reached into his back pocket for some Flexicuffs and glance toward Fred. "Can you cuff her?"

Fred nodded, then tried to rise. He didn't make it. "Give me a second," he gasped.

"I can do it," Laurel said. "Fred took a huge blow to his head."

Cade tossed the Flexicuffs toward Laurel.

He rolled off the woman and wrapped his left hand around the nape of the her neck.

"I can shoot you or I can break your neck," he said calmly. "Your choice."

She didn't move.

Laurel crawled over and picked up the Flexicuffs. She pulled the woman's unresisting hands together and cuffed her.

Cade relaxed a little once the woman's hands were cuffed, but he didn't take her for granted. She'd pack a hell of a wallop with a head-butt or a well-placed kick.

He stood. "Get up!" He hooked a hand around her elbow and jerked her up. "You're under arrest for assaulting a federal officer. You have the right to remain silent and anything you say may be used against you in a court of law."

"No, wait. I just wanted to scare her—stop her from digging into Wendell's death."

Laurel gasped. "I know you. You're Sheryl Posey. You're one of the CeeGees. You really did kill Wendell, didn't you? You and the other CeeGees."

"No! We put that sign to his back at the graduation

ceremony, but Kathy and Debra weren't satisfied. Debra lured him out to the creek bank. She gave him this whole line about how she thought a smart man was so sexy."

"And Wendell believed her? After everything the CeeGees had done?"

Sheryl shrugged. "He was eighteen. And Debra was really cute. He let her lure him out here. Kathy hid while I sneaked up behind him and yanked the chain of the science medal from around his neck. We were going to make him take off all his clothes before we'd give it back." She jerked against Cade's hold. "But the chain didn't break right away. It choked him and he passed out. Deb and Kathy got totally spooked. They were afraid he was dead."

"But he wasn't," Laurel said.

"No! I swear! The chain must have pressed on something vital. He went out like a light, but he was still breathing."

Cade had heard enough. "Let's go. I'm taking you in on suspicion of murder." He took her by the arm.

"Wait!" She strained against his grip. "You don't understand. I didn't kill anybody."

"We'll see."

Sheryl shook her head, then eyed Cade. "I'm not going down for this. I helped humiliate Wendell, but I'm not the one that killed him. If I give you his killer, will you let me go—give me some kind of immunity?"

"Depends on what you've got."

"Good." She relaxed a little. "But listen, we've got to hurry."

"Why?"

Sheryl turned to look at Laurel. "Because the real killer will be here in a few minutes."

"The real killer? Who?" Laurel asked.

A loud crack shattered the still morning air. A gunshot. For an instant everything stopped.

Then Cade heard a yelp of pain, and Sheryl and Laurel both collapsed onto the ground.

Chapter Twelve

Laurel! Cade dove to the ground as a second shot rang out. He whirled and fired in the direction the shots came from—the rise on the opposite bank of the creek. But there was nobody there. Whoever had fired the shot was gone.

He crawled across the damp ground toward Laurel. She and Sheryl were both sprawled on the ground. Sheryl was lying facedown across Laurel's feet, blood spreading across the back of her tank top. He couldn't tell whether the bullet had pierced her heart or not. It was certainly close.

Beneath her, Laurel lay unmoving, her eyes closed and her arms flung out. Her right hand and forearm were smeared with blood.

Dear God, don't let her be hurt. By the time he got to her, she'd opened her eyes.

"Are you hit?" he demanded, brushing dirt from her face. She shook her head. "What happened?"

Cade shed his shirt and bunched it against Sheryl's wound, praying that when he turned her over, there wouldn't be a gaping exit wound in her chest. There wasn't.

He positioned her so that her weight pressed her back against the shirt. As he did, Laurel slid her legs out from under her.

Sheryl whispered something.

"Sheryl, don't talk," Cade said. "I'm calling an ambulance."

"Ralph—" She gasped. "Watch out for—" Her voice trailed off.

"Save your energy." He couldn't tell how badly she was hurt. The bullet was still inside her and he had no way of knowing where it had lodged. "You're going to be fine. I'll get an ambulance."

He dug his cell phone out of his pocket.

"Cade!" Fred exclaimed. "Look out."

He whirled toward Fred just as Laurel's voice came from behind him.

"C-Cade—" She sounded terrified. He looked toward her. What he saw turned his heart to ice in his chest.

Ralph Langston was standing behind Laurel, his left forearm tight around her throat, his right hand holding a gun to the side of her neck.

Cade's mouth went dry. "Langston—" he croaked. Sheryl had been trying to warn him. She knew Langston was coming.

"Drop the gun and the phone."

Cade did his best to put aside the paralyzing fear that Ralph would shoot Laurel. "Let her go," he said, forcing himself to speak in a commanding tone. "If Sheryl lives, I'll testify that you cooperated."

"Sheryl? You think I shot her?" Ralph laughed. "I wish— but it wasn't me. That shot came from across the creek. I couldn't get over here that fast. Now do what I said."

Cade didn't move from his crouched position.

Ralph dug the barrel of the gun into Laurel's neck until she whimpered with pain. "Do it."

"Sheryl's going to die if I don't call for help." Cade was exaggerating, but he'd tell Ralph anything to save Laurel.

Ralph squeezed Laurel's throat. She grabbed on to his forearm with her left hand, struggling to breathe.

Cade saw blood dripping from Laurel's right hand. Had she caught a bullet after all?

"Do I look like I care? Sheryl was black—" He stopped.

"Blackmailing you? Is that what you were going to say? Why? Because you killed Wendell? That's what she told me."

"She wouldn't tell you that."

"Langston, put the gun down. What the hell do you think you're going to accomplish? You're just buying yourself a date with a needle."

"Please tell me you know I'm not that stupid."

"You set fire to the police station. You had to destroy the evidence because you knew it would prove you'd killed Debra. The fibers under her nails are from your fancy custom-made slacks. Not to mention the mud that proves you were down by the Swinging Oak."

Cade threw that out in desperation. He had no idea what the evidence would support. All he had was a bluff. He prayed it was enough to save Laurel's life.

"You killed my girl?" Fred yelled. "You killed Debra? I ought to—"

Ralph swung his gun toward Fred. "You shut up or I'll shut you up for good." He took a step backward and swung Laurel around so he could see both Cade and Fred.

Then he turned the gun back on Laurel, jabbing it into her neck with a vengeance that Cade knew would leave a bruise. But a bruised neck was the least of his concerns for her. He'd take a bruise any day, as long as he could have her back safe in his arms.

Ralph's hand tightened on the gun and Laurel's face grew more and more pale.

Cade tossed his phone down, but he wasn't about to relinquish his weapon. Not without a fight. He rose to his feet.

Ralph jerked in surprise. "I said drop the gun," he yelled.

"What are you doing, Langston? Are you going to shoot all three of us? Because if you shoot Laurel I'll make sure you never walk again."

"You shut up. Everything's out of control and it's all her fault."

Laurel coughed. Ralph was choking her.

Cade took careful aim, holding his gun in two hands. Could he take the shot? Could he risk hitting Laurel to stop Ralph? If he didn't risk it, Ralph would kill her.

And if that happened… His gun hand wavered. He gritted his teeth and concentrated on the gun barrel against her neck.

Stop him. Save her. That's all he could afford to think about. If he let go of the iron-fisted control he had on his emotions, he'd lose it, and Laurel wouldn't have a chance.

He could *not* love her—he couldn't care more about saving her than he did about anyone in his town.

"So if you didn't shoot Sheryl, who's your partner across the creek? And why do y'all want Sheryl dead? Are you afraid she'll talk?"

Cade had no clue what Sheryl had been about to tell him. He was betting everything that she'd come upon Langston killing Wendell. *Everything.*

There was only one reason Ralph would threaten to kill Laurel. He couldn't let her keep digging into Wendell's death.

"You thought you could get away with it, didn't you?" Cade had to say enough to make Ralph nervous, but not enough to tip him off that he had no clue what he was talking about.

"You're not going to trick me into talking." Ralph's eyes darted back and forth between Fred and Cade. Fred had pushed himself to his knees and was shaking his head. Ralph pointed the gun's barrel at him, then realized what he'd done and turned it back on Laurel.

Cade felt a grim satisfaction. He was getting to him. "I don't have to. Sheryl told me all I need to know."

Ralph's eyes flickered down at Sheryl then back up. "No, she didn't. She wouldn't. She'd be—" He took a shaky breath. "She wouldn't."

But Ralph didn't believe his own words. His voice was shrill with worry. And he was sweating. Cade almost had him.

"Anyhow, she's dead," Ralph cried.

"No, she's not. But even if she dies, I've got everything she said on tape." He patted his shirt pocket, hoping the other man was too shaken to notice there was not the slightest bulge there. "So no matter what happens to her, I've got you. Don't make it worse. Put that gun down before it goes off."

"What?" Ralph screamed. "What did she tell you?"

Cade shrugged. "Enough."

"You don't have anything. If you did you'd tell me." He jerked his arm, cutting off Laurel's breath completely.

Cade's heart shattered as he watched Laurel struggle for air.

Time had run out.

Cade squeezed the gun's handle and lined up the sights with the center of Ralph's forehead. He had no idea if Ralph would actually shoot Laurel. All he knew was that as much as he wished it was otherwise, he'd never be able to get a fatal shot off before Ralph pulled the trigger.

His mouth went dry. He had to play his trump card. If he was wrong, it could mean Laurel's death. "You killed Wendell. You took his medal, and Sheryl saw you." He tensed, his finger poised over the trigger.

Ralph's remolded face looked like it was melting. "You don't know that. You can't." He switched his gaze to the ground, to Sheryl. "You can't!"

Cade saw Ralph's knuckles turn white around the gun. His heart bounced up into his throat and hammered wildly. Just as Cade was ready to take the hard shot, Ralph pulled Laurel closer and angled his body so that she blocked him almost entirely. There was no way Cade could shoot without hitting her.

LAUREL'S HEART POUNDED with panic. She couldn't get enough air. She was losing her grip on consciousness. Her vision was already turning black. She struggled to breathe. Struggled to think.

She knew Ralph had the advantage. Her fists clenched in helpless rage. A sharp pain ripped through her right hand and sticky liquid squeezed out between her fingers. The glass shard!

The pain in her foot earlier had been that shard stabbing into the flesh behind her ankle. She'd had to pull the damn thing out. It was sharp as hell.

She'd forgotten she was still holding it.

Ralph's arm relaxed a bit, enough for her to breathe. She gulped in a huge lungful of air.

His arm muscles flexed and panic squeezed her chest again. She didn't have long. Staring at Cade, she willed him to look at her.

Finally his gaze met hers briefly. If she'd had breath, the look in that hot blue gaze would have sucked it right out of her. He knew she was going to die.

She cut her eyes to the side, hoping he'd get the message.

He did. His blue eyes widened and his jaw bulged with tension. He gave his head a shake—almost unnoticeable.

But Laurel knew it was their last chance. Their only chance.

Squeezing the piece of glass between her fingers, she bent her elbow like a spring and stabbed Ralph in his gun arm.

He screeched. A shot rang out.

She dove for the ground and rolled away from Ralph as Cade rushed him and tackled him. He slammed him down to the ground.

"I'm bleeding! I'm dying!" Ralph cried. "You shot me!"

"Shut up," Cade growled as he jerked Ralph's arms behind him and cuffed him. "The bullet barely grazed your shoulder. You'll live to stand trial."

Laurel's breath caught in a sob of relief as Cade quickly read Ralph his rights. Maybe it was finally over.

Cade turned to her. "Laurel, honey. Are you okay?"

"I think so." She rolled over and sat up. "What about Fred? And Sheryl?"

"You're bleeding," he croaked.

She looked down. The hem of her jeans and the whole side of her tennis shoe was soaked with blood. "A lot of that is Sheryl's blood. But I did step on a piece of glass." She stuck her leg out. "Oh, yeah, I cut my hand, too."

"You stabbed Ralph with that piece of glass?"

"It was all I had," she said as she pushed herself up off the ground.

Cade scrutinized Laurel closely. Satisfied that she was okay, he went to check on Fred, who was pushing himself up to his feet.

"Sorry, Cade," Fred muttered, holding a hand to his bleeding head. "I let a bump on the head keep me from helping you."

"Looks to me like that's quite a blow. You might need some stitches."

"Nah. I'm fine. I'll take Ralph in for you." He glanced around and spotted his weapon a few feet away. He retrieved and holstered it.

"Okay, but I'm going to get the EMTs down here to look at everybody. You make sure they check out your head."

"Sure thing, Cade." Fred grabbed Langston's arm.

Cade pulled out his cell phone and dialed Kit Haydel. "Hey, Kit, I need the EMTs down here at the creek bank. Got several injuries. Hurry."

Then he called Shelton to bring the crime-scene kit. He pocketed his phone and bent over Sheryl. He felt for her pulse. It was weak but steady. He did his best to staunch the bleeding.

Within five minutes, the EMTs showed up. They took over Sheryl's care, hanging an IV and carrying her out of the clearing on a stretcher. Fred went with them, guarding Langston. Cade sent Laurel over to have them tend to her ankle and hand.

For the moment, he was alone. He leaned against the Swinging Oak, shaky with relief now that the danger was over.

He wiped his face and gave in to the abject fear that had taken hold of him when he'd seen the gun at Laurel's throat. He clenched his fists. She'd nearly died, and the whole time she'd looked to him to save her.

He hadn't known there was that much fear inside him. Or that much love.

"Crap," he muttered. What the hell was he doing—falling for her? She'd be heading back to D.C. as soon as she could.

Oh, she'd have to stay around for a few days. There would be paperwork to complete, evidence to process and statements to take before she could leave. But none of that would take long. He predicted Langston wouldn't survive an hour of intense questioning before breaking down. They'd have a signed confession before dark. They might not even need the evidence, except to confirm Ralph's story.

He heard footsteps. He cleared his throat and straightened, still clutching his weapon. He watched the path to see who was coming.

It was one of Kit's voluntary firemen. He carried the camera and the crime-scene kit.

"Hey, Joe. What're you doing with that stuff? Where's Shelton?" Cade asked him.

"He called Chief Haydel and asked him to get the kit and the camera over here to you. Apparently Shelton had an accident."

"An accident? Is he all right?"

The fireman nodded. "The chief told me Kathy Adler ran into him."

"Oh, yeah?" Cade perked up.

"Apparently she plowed into the side of the squad car, then took off in that monster SUV of hers. The collision ripped a tire so he couldn't drive it. The Chief said to tell you she was coming from the direction of the Visitor Center."

Cade's brain raced. So Kathy had been in the vicinity of the Visitor Center right around the time Sheryl Posey was shot.

Had Kathy shot her? Ralph had certainly been telling the truth about that. There was no way he could have shot Sheryl and then made it around to the clearing so fast.

Cade took the camera and kit from Joe and thanked him.

"No problem, sir. Need me to stick around and help?"

"No," Cade said. "Go ahead." He quickly processed the crime scene and taped it off. While he was working, Shelton called and asked if everyone was okay.

Cade filled him in.

"Well, if that don't beat all, Cade," Shelton said. "I'm heading over to Mrs. Adler's house in my pickup. I figure she'll go home eventually, if she doesn't wrap herself around a tree first."

"Be careful," Cade warned him. "She may be armed."

"Armed? Kathy Adler?"

"Several shots came from the rise over near the Visitor Center. Kathy could have been involved in the shooting."

"Is this connected to Fred's girl's death?"

"I'm afraid so. When you question Kathy about the collision, don't mention the shooting. I don't have any proof yet."

"You got it, boss."

Cade hung up, took one last glance around the cordoned-off crime scene, and then headed up the path toward his truck. Just as he rounded the last curve of the path, a soft, firm, sweet-smelling someone ran into him.

It was Laurel. He reached out to steady her and caught her bandaged hand.

She winced.

"Sorry," he muttered. He looked her over from head to toe. She looked a hundred percent better than she had a few minutes ago. The EMTs had bandaged her ankle and her hand. She'd managed to wash her face, getting her hair damp in the process. It curled around her face. She looked fresh and sweet and tired, and very unlike an FBI agent. His heart twisted but he ignored it.

"Stitches?"

She looked at her hand. "A couple."

"I thought you were going to the hospital with the EMTs."

"My car's here."

"Right. I'm supposed to believe they released you?"

She waved a hand. "I told them I was fine."

"So they didn't release you." His voice was gruffer than

he intended it to be, but he couldn't shake the vision of her with Langston's gun buried in her neck.

She could have been killed because he hadn't had the foresight to put his damn cell phone on vibrate.

Right now he was feeling exposed and vulnerable. He wasn't ready to make apologies and admit how afraid he'd been that he couldn't save her.

So he decided the best defense was a strong offense. "Why the hell did you leave the house after I told you not to?"

"Because Sheryl called and told me someone was going to kill her."

"You fell for that? You should have waited for me."

"I didn't *fall* for anything, Dupree. After what happened to Debra, I couldn't risk waiting. For all I knew you were trapped in the fire or shot by whoever *lured* you out. When I couldn't reach you, I called Fred to meet me at the parking lot, but he didn't wait. He came down here by himself and Sheryl got the drop on him. He managed to knock the gun out of her hand, but then she conked him with the tree branch."

"Sorry I didn't hear your call. The sirens were blasting and the fire was roaring—"

Laurel held up a hand. "You got here in time. But what I want to know is—why didn't you take the shot?"

Cade couldn't meet her gaze right then. If he did, she'd know why. Trying to protect his heart, he gave her the stock answer. "I couldn't get a clean shot."

"That's bull. You had him before he twisted. You should have taken it."

"We'll have to agree to disagree on that one, Special Agent Gillespie."

She frowned. "Fine. If you'll let me know when you plan to be back at your place, I'll swing by and get my stuff. I should move back to the bed-and-breakfast."

Cade saw the shadows in her hazel eyes. Did she want him to ask her to stay? Because he couldn't. Not now that he knew how he felt about her. He'd had relationships—a couple of fairly serious ones—but he'd never felt like this before.

He didn't know how to deal with it.

"You don't have to move out," he muttered.

Her gaze faltered. "I think it's best."

She sounded cold as ice. Did she regret what had happened between them now that the danger was over?

"I'll run by and let you in. Then I have to question Ralph and deal with Kathy."

"Kathy?"

He nodded wearily. "Yeah. She was speeding and ran her car into the squad car and then left the scene. Shelton said she was coming from the direction of the Visitor Center."

Laurel's eyes shone. "Really? Oh, my gosh, it was Kathy who shot Sheryl?"

"Looks like it."

"I have *got* to hear what she has to say. She's up to her ears in this mess."

He nodded. "I agree. But you should take it easy—"

She stepped in front of him, her back stiff. "Look, Dupree, I don't need to take it easy. I can handle myself. So I'd appreciate it if you wouldn't try to tell me what to do." She turned and stalked down the path toward the parking area.

Her indignant stalk would have been more impressive and less amusing if she hadn't been limping, but oddly, Cade didn't feel like smiling. To his chagrin, the lump was back in his throat.

Chapter Thirteen

Laurel packed her suitcase for the third time in the three days she'd been in Dusty Springs. This time was the hardest, and not because her right hand was bandaged.

She stopped in the middle of zipping her suitcase and stared at the open bedroom door. Her heart squeezed so tightly in her chest that it physically hurt.

Cade had made love to her in that room. He'd held her and touched her and filled her with an ecstasy akin to nothing she'd ever felt before. She'd finally gotten the one thing she'd always wanted. *Cade Dupree.*

Back when she was sixteen, she'd been sure that if he'd just pay attention to her, her life would be complete.

Well, he'd paid attention to her. Plenty of attention. And when she left here this time, she wouldn't just be leaving behind a schoolgirl crush. She'd be leaving her heart.

She walked over to the bedroom door. The unmade bed still held the imprint of their bodies. She couldn't leave it like that. It would be like leaving a love note behind. She straightened the sheets and the blanket, letting her hands linger on the pillows. She felt the sting of tears. Her throat ached. Coming back to Dusty Springs had let her realize a dream. The fact that she'd be leaving the dream behind was probably fitting.

Cade had only known her for three days. Prior to that, she'd been nothing but a face in a yearbook. He couldn't possibly care for her as much as she cared for him. He was part of her past. It was probably best that he remain there.

Tears slipped down her cheeks, but that was okay. It was only natural to cry at goodbyes.

She walked around the bed to smooth one last wrinkle and almost knocked her knee on the bedside table drawer. It was ajar. She started to push it shut but the edge of a framed picture caught her eye.

Oh, no. Don't go snooping.

She was going to look. Yes, she really had sunk that low. Cade was at Three Springs Hospital, checking on Sheryl and Ralph. There was no way he would be back any time soon.

Disgusted with herself, she slid the drawer open. The picture was of Cade's high school graduation. Cade's dad had his arm around Cade's shoulder and Cade was looking at him with pride and love. On his dad's other side, James's gaze lingered somewhere beyond the range of the camera. He looked terminally bored.

"Oh, Cade," she whispered, sitting down on the edge of the bed. "You were never in James's shadow." She started to put the picture back in the drawer. But something else caught her eye. An open envelope with the FBI's seal on it.

Close the drawer, she commanded herself. But instead she reached for the envelope. Great, Gillespie. You're officially a stalker now.

She slid the sheets of paper out of the envelope and unfolded them. It was his assignment letter from the FBI.

Speaking of dreams left behind. Holding her breath to keep from sobbing, she scanned it quickly.

A noise penetrated her brain. It was a key turning in the front door lock. She froze.

Busted.

Do it, she commanded herself. Toss the envelope and picture back into the drawer, kick it shut and pretend to be making the bed.

But she couldn't move as footsteps crossed the hardwood floor.

"Laurel!"

"Mr. Dupree!" It was Cade's dad.

"I didn't expect to see you here."

"I—I shouldn't be. I'm packing to leave right now."

He eyed the letter in her hand. "So Cade tells me y'all may have cracked the case."

"I think so. As soon as we get the evidence back from the FBI lab, we should be able to wrap it up. Sheryl Posey gave Cade her statement this morning. She witnessed Ralph choking Wendell before he strung him up."

She spoke nervously and quickly. It took a lot of will-power not to hide the hand holding Cade's FBI letter behind her back.

"We're sure that the fibers under Debra's nails will turn out to be a match for Ralph's pants. Luckily he wears custom-tailored suits, so the match should be easy. If they're a match, we should have him on two counts of murder—Debra's and Wendell Vance's."

Mr. Dupree nodded. "Sounds like everything's working out fine. So—" He smiled. "Wha-cha got there?"

"I—uh—" she stammered.

"You were snooping?" he asked.

Her face burned like fire. Looking down at her feet, she nodded.

"It's only natural. You're a cop. It's what we do. So wha'd you find?"

Mr. Dupree stepped forward and took the envelope from her fingers. His smile faded and he shook his head. "I wanted to tell Cade he didn't have to give up the FBI and come back here, but the first few weeks after my stroke I couldn't talk at all. I never expected him to take over my job. I always thought Fred would be Chief after me."

"What about James?"

Mr. Dupree looked up. "You never knew James, did you?"

"No." She didn't bother telling him about her humiliating experience and James's part in it.

"That boy could charm anybody into doin' anything. Never listened to anybody. Never thought there was anything he couldn't do."

Laurel's heart was throbbing with pain. Pain for the man who'd lost his first-born son. Pain for his living son, who'd never been able to make up for James dying.

"I'm sure you were devastated when he died."

"Yes. But it was typical James. He was hot-shotting in a helicopter and crashed."

"Oh. I'm so sorry."

Mr. Dupree smiled sadly. "He thought he was immortal."

Laurel's heart squeezed in sympathy. She dropped her gaze, and saw what he had in his hand. A box of dark chocolate-covered cherries.

"So you're leaving?" he asked.

"I think I'd better."

"Maybe so."

Laurel stared at him in surprise.

"All I'm saying is Cade takes everything to heart. He doesn't deserve to be hurt. And he's the only son I have left."

Laurel drew in courage with a deep breath. "Why do you call him that, Mr. Dupree?"

"'Cause that's what he is. It reminds me that he's the most precious thing in my life." He smiled at her.

"Does he know he is?" she asked.

The elder Dupree looked thoughtful. "I always thought so. But considering the chocolate cherry misunderstanding, maybe I need to talk to him, too."

"The chocolate cherry misunderstanding?"

Mr. Dupree lifted a hand. "Never mind. It's a long story."

Laurel smiled sadly. "I think I know the gist of it."

He frowned at her. "Oh, yeah? Maybe you know my boy better than I thought you did."

Maybe. Laurel's heart twisted painfully. "Thank you for everything, Mr. Dupree—"

"Dad—"

Laurel whirled at the sharp word.

Cade stood in the open door. He looked from his dad to Laurel and back.

"What the hell?" he asked, glaring at his dad.

"Cade, this is my fault," Laurel started, but his dad interrupted her.

"Son, I brought you something. And Laurel and I were talking about the case—and the FBI."

"Dad—" Cade's pained voice held a warning.

Mr. Dupree sent Laurel a glance. Understanding, she slipped around them and headed for the front door. Behind her, she heard Cade.

"Dark chocolate cherries? What the hell? I thought they were James's favorite."

"As I recall, you loved 'em, but you'd never fight James. You always let him bully you."

Laurel pulled out her cell phone and dialed a familiar

number. She had an important question to ask her boss, Mitch Decker.

As she eased the door closed, she heard Mr. Dupree's voice change.

"Cade, son," he said. "We need to talk."

THE NEXT MORNING, Cade was up early. He hadn't been able to sleep the night before. He'd been shocked and angry when he'd found his dad and Laurel in his house. They'd gone through his stuff. They'd talked about him. He felt betrayed by both of them.

Damn Laurel for coming back here and turning his life upside down. He'd forgotten about the FBI. He'd been happy back in Dusty Springs before she showed up.

He was a liar. It hadn't taken her to remind him of everything he'd given up. She'd just emphasized how long it had been. He always thought that one day he'd go back and pick up where he'd left off when James died.

But meeting Laurel made him realize he'd not only put his dreams on hold, he'd put his whole life on hold. Hell, he rarely even dated anymore.

He'd done it all for his dad, but yesterday evening his dad informed him in no uncertain terms that he didn't need Cade's constant attention. He'd told him a lot of other things, too. Things they should have talked about years ago.

Things guys would rather have a root canal than discuss. But at least now Cade knew his dad was okay. For the first time since James died, Cade let himself think about *his* dreams.

There were two things he wanted, and he was afraid it was too late for both of them.

Cade showered, taunted by Laurel's lingering fresh scent. Even though she'd taken all her belongings and moved back to the bed-and-breakfast, he could still smell gardenias. How long would it take for the sweet scent to fade from his bathroom? A part of him wanted it gone today, but his heart hoped it would stay forever.

After pulling on jeans and a T-shirt, he grabbed a baseball cap. He needed to go over to the hospital at Three Springs and arrange for Ralph to be transferred to the jail to await a bail hearing, but first he wanted to check on the mess that had been the police station.

The entire front of the station was nothing but sodden rubble. Here and there an anemic wisp of smoke drifted upward through the air.

The desk his grandfather and his father had used was destroyed. All the papers on current cases, all the case files were ruined. Thank goodness Wendell Vance's file was still at his house. The evidence room was intact, although everything inside it would smell like smoke forever.

He picked his way back out through the rubble, wishing he'd worn his old running shoes instead of his new ones. As he emerged through the burnt-out front of the building, he saw Ralph Langston, looking very much the victim with his arm in a sling. He was accompanied by a man in a gray pinstriped suit who looked like a lawyer.

What the hell? Cade got a sinking feeling in his chest. How had the lawyer managed to get Ralph out of the hospital and away from the Three Springs police who were guarding his door?

"What's going on here? Langston, you're supposed to be in police custody."

"Good morning, Chief Dupree," the lawyer said. "I'm Arnold Griffon, Mr. Langston's lawyer. As a matter of fact, he has a perfect right to be out of jail. He's posted bail."

"Posted bail—on a federal assault charge?"

The lawyer chuckled. "I'm very good friends with a judge who was happy to order bail in the amount of one hundred thousand dollars."

Cade clenched his jaw against the anger that burned in his gut. Langston had threatened Laurel's life. He didn't deserve to walk free for an instant. "So you neglected to tell your *good friend* that your client here assaulted a federal officer."

Griffon didn't answer. "I believe someone brought Mr. Langston's belongings here from the hospital last night. He's anxious to get them back."

"Not a chance. They contain evidence that links Langston directly to Wendell Vance's death." To Cade's satisfaction the lawyer looked surprised.

He turned to Ralph. "Who's Wendell Vance?"

"He's got nothing," Ralph squawked.

"Are you calling Wendell Vance's Science Medal nothing? I doubt you felt that way when you took it off his body after you killed him ten years ago on the night of your graduation."

"That's a lie," Ralph said.

Cade turned to the lawyer. "Wendell Vance was a classmate of Ralph's who was murdered on graduation night ten years ago. His science medal disappeared. Turns out your client here has it. He carries it around in a leather wallet, like it belongs to him."

Cade felt a keen triumph when the red faded from Griffon's face. "Didn't your client tell you that one of the *belongings* he wants to pick up is that science medal?"

The lawyer literally put a finger to his shirt collar and swallowed visibly. "I'd like to speak to my client alone for a few minutes, Chief."

"Be my guest. I suppose you'd like to step into our private offices?" Cade made a sweeping gesture that encompassed the burnt-out police station.

Just then, a truck turned onto the street. It was a FedEx truck. Cade grinned. "Here comes the rest of our evidence now."

Langston sent a panicked look at the truck as he followed Griffon to a point a few yards away.

Cade couldn't believe the evidence had been returned so quickly. When he was handed the package, he saw that it hadn't. The delivery was a bulletin of missing children in the region. It came once a month.

He glanced over at Langston. They didn't have to know that, though. Let them think he had solid evidence in his hands. Both of them eyed him and then moved further away.

Another vehicle turned onto the street. It was Laurel. Cade recognized her rental car. His stomach did a flip. Immediately, he convinced himself that it hadn't—almost.

She got out of her car, limping slightly.

He couldn't look her in the eye. He'd been too exposed the other day—too vulnerable. She didn't look directly at him, either.

"Oh, Cade," she said, eyeing the wreckage that had been the police station. "The whole building is destroyed."

"Not quite. The evidence room is intact."

She looked at him then. "I'm glad." Her cheeks turned pink. "What's Langston doing out of the hospital?"

"His big-city lawyer had Langston arraigned in the middle of the night. He posted bail."

Cade bent his head to whisper in her ear—a mistake. He withdrew and told himself gardenias were way overrated. "Guess what turned up in his belongings," he said.

Her eyes blazed with color. "Not the medal?"

"Yes, the medal. He had a leather wallet made special for it. He carried it around like a police badge."

"Oh, my gosh. You mean he's carried it with him all these years?"

"Yep. That confirms what Sheryl told me this morning."

"She *was* trying to say Ralph was Wendell's killer."

Cade laid a hand on her arm. "Whoa. Slow down. It proves he was at the crime scene and took the medal. If Sheryl's statement holds up and the evidence bears it out, *then* we can get him for Wendell's murder."

"What about her? Was it Kathy who shot her?"

"The bullet the hospital took out of her shoulder has an L on it."

"I knew it! And get this. Mitch called. He's sending first pass results of the fingerprint IDs by special courier. Kathy's prints matched partials on Misty's baseball bat and her TV remote, the inside doorknob of my room at the bed-and-breakfast and that slug I dug out of the tree. *And* on the key Debra was carrying. She was the one trying to steal the photos."

"What else did Mitch say?"

"No other significant fingerprint matches. But the fibers under Debra's nails matched the swatch of fabric from Ralph's pants leg."

Cade's brows rose. "Good. That makes him the prime suspect for killing Debra, too. When I present that evidence to his lawyer, he'll be begging for a plea agreement, rather than twenty-five years to life in a federal penitentiary. I hope you told your boss how much I appreciate it. That was damn fast work. And damn fine."

"Mitch Decker can get the job done."

And so can you. Cade silently acknowledged Laurel's bravery and dedication. She'd nearly been killed twice. It had taken seven stitches on her palm and foot to repair the damage done by the glass shard, and yet she hadn't faltered.

He remembered how much seeing her weapon tucked in the small of her back had turned him on. Now he realized it wasn't the sight of the gun sitting above the curve of her bottom that had caused that reaction. It was what it represented.

Strength, competence, courage. Those were the qualities that turned him on and made him love her. Not that her sexy body and gorgeous eyes hurt.

He realized she was gazing at him quizzically, a tiny frown marring her forehead.

He cleared his throat and searched for something innocuous to say. "I got to tell you, Gillespie, arresting Langston is going to be a pleasure."

His last word was drowned out by a loud roar. It was Kathy's dark SUV. She screeched to a halt so close to them that Cade wrapped an arm around Laurel's waist and pulled her clear.

As soon as the SUV stopped, Kathy shot out of it like her legs were spring-loaded. She stomped over to Cade, clutching her open purse in one hand and a nearly burned-down cigarette in the other.

"Cade, Shelton told me you needed to see me. I know I'm in big trouble, but I want to confess everything and ask for your protection. I'm the one who took Laurel's gun." Kathy's voice was shrill, her eyes were too bright and her movements were jerky.

Cade couldn't decide if she was drunk or on some sort of drug.

"See, Cade, I had to get those pictures. They proved we killed Wendell. Sheryl always said we didn't, that he was alive when we left, but Ralph told us Wendell was dead. And ever since that night, he—" She stopped.

"Kathy, where's Harrison?" Cade asked. "You need to

get a lawyer. You realize I can arrest you for assaulting a federal officer, based on what you've just told me. *And* go after you for Wendell's murder."

"I know that. I only meant to scare Laurel off the case, so she wouldn't find out what we'd done. I'm so tired…" She took a shaky breath. "Cade, I shot Sheryl. I was *so* sure she'd killed Debra. I saw her near the path to the swimming hole the night of the reunion, right before Debra was found. I've been following her ever since. I followed her to the creek bank—" She glanced past him and stopped cold.

"Oh, my God! What's he doing—what are you doing here?" she yelled at Langston. "If you think you're going to—" She tossed away the cigarette butt and dug into her voluminous purse.

Cade tensed and flexed his fingers. Out of the corner of his eye he saw Laurel move stealthily backward, position-ing herself behind Kathy. The white bandage on her hand stood out in stark contrast to her green top and jeans.

"Kathy," he said calmly. "Don't get upset. Let's talk about this."

"There's nothing to talk about. That man ruined my life."

Langston and his lawyer were moving closer. They must not have heard Kathy's outburst—or they were idiots and didn't see how agitated she was.

Cade couldn't even spare them a glance. He had to keep all his attention on Kathy.

"Kathy, take your hand out of your purse." Cade reached toward her but she jerked away violently.

"No! I'm finishing this here and now."

"Kathy—"

But Kathy wasn't listening to him.

"You monster—" That was aimed at Langston. "You've held Wendell's death over me for the past ten years! But not anymore!" She pulled a gun out of her purse and waved it wildly.

Langston grabbed his lawyer's arm and tried to push him in front of him as Kathy leveled the gun at him and held it in both hands like a pro.

"I used up every bit of my inheritance paying you hush money for ten years. And Debra drained her parents and made them think she was a spendthrift. You made our lives hell." She glanced at Cade. "Then when Laurel started nosing around, he threatened to tell you we killed Wendell unless I got the pictures and stopped her. It had been ten years. Everybody had accepted Wendell's death as suicide. But Ralph didn't want to lose his gravy train. Greedy, heartless—!"

"Kathy," Cade said quietly. "You didn't kill Wendell."

"What?" She turned her head toward Cade. "What are you talking about?"

Cade let his gaze drift behind her where Laurel had her backup weapon in her hand and was slowly creeping closer to Kathy.

He'd been taking a step every time Laurel did, but Langston's lawyer had parked his car right in front of the burnt-out station house. It was in Cade's way. He had to detour around it.

"Kathy," he said. "Let's talk about this. Why don't you give me the gun so you don't make things worse for yourself. I know you didn't kill Wendell. He was unconscious but he wasn't dead when you left him."

"Didn't kill—? But Ralph blackmailed us for ten years." She shot a wild-eyed look at Cade. "And it was for *nothing?*"

He stopped and tried to look harmless. "I'll tell you all about it if you'll give me the gun."

She took another step toward Langston. "You knew about this?"

Langston was white as a sheet. He took a step backward. "I swear, Kathy, I thought you killed him."

"You are a liar! You told us you found Wendell dead. You said you'd hanged him to make it look like suicide— to protect *us*. Oh, my God, you killed him." Kathy laughed. "And Sheryl knew, didn't she? She was as greedy as you. Maybe I'm not sorry I shot her, after all."

"No, I swear! I saw Wendell and Debra headed toward the swimming hole. I knew y'all had more cooked up for him than a sign on his back. Did I want to see Wendell humiliated? Yes. Did I kill him? No!"

Laurel moved toward Kathy, staying out of her line of sight. Cade saw her release the safety on her gun. *Good. Keep closing in on her.* Laurel was doing exactly the right things.

With stiff, jerky motions, Kathy moved away from Cade and toward the other side of the street. She hadn't yet become aware of Laurel behind her.

Cade stayed in step with her, and within ten steps, he was closer to Langston and the lawyer than she was.

"Kathy, we're going to take care of Langston," Cade said, deliberately keeping his voice quiet and calm. "He'll pay for everything he's done. You don't want to shoot him."

"Kathy," Langston choked out. "I swear to God I'm telling the truth. Maybe Sheryl killed Wendell herself—"

"You," Kathy shrieked, "shut your lying mouth. I dealt with Sheryl and I'll deal with you!"

Cade didn't like the look in Kathy's eyes or the hysterical tone in her voice. He aimed his weapon in her direction.

She saw him.

"He killed Wendell, Cade! He killed him and he blackmailed us!"

"Kathy," Cade said. "Set the gun down and we'll talk."

"No! You tell me or I'll shoot him, right here."

"Come on, Kathy, you don't want to shoot him. Sheryl's going to be okay. You haven't killed anyone."

"You can't stop me. I have to do this," she cried. "I've lived in fear for ten years."

As if in slow motion, Cade saw her finger squeeze the trigger. He had to make the right decision within microseconds now or someone would die.

He sent a quick glance in Laurel's direction, then dove toward Langston and the lawyer, pushing them down.

Cade felt like he was moving in slow motion as several loud pops sounded in his ears. Something hit him with a wallop, and he slammed into the hot pavement and rolled.

Langston screamed. The lawyer whimpered. Laurel yelled at Kathy.

Cade rolled up into a crouch. Laurel had knocked Kathy to her knees and was cuffing her. The FBI issue Glock that Kathy had held lay on the ground beside her.

Cade sprang to his feet and ran to Ralph's side. He knelt and felt for a pulse. *Nothing.* One of Kathy's shots had hit him. Cade lifted his left arm to reach into his pocket for his cell phone, but to his surprise, it didn't do what he wanted it to. He glanced down. Blood spread like an opening flower on his yellow pullover shirt.

He set his gun down, retrieved his phone and called the EMTs. Kathy was beginning to calm down somewhat, but she was still threatening to kill Langston. She didn't realize he was already dead.

"Cade? Are you okay?" Laurel called out, her voice tight with concern.

He met her gaze and nodded.

In her eyes he read the same thing he was thinking. It was over, but not soon enough. Too many lives had been destroyed.

IT WAS TIME to leave. There was nothing else for Laurel to do. Cade had everything well in hand. The day before had been an odd mixture of terror and boredom. It had ended with Ralph Langston dead, Cade injured and Kathy Adler's life in shambles.

Kathy's confession had cleared up a lot of unanswered questions. Then, after Cade's shoulder was bandaged and he was released from the hospital, he'd filled Laurel in on what Sheryl had told him.

The whole thing was so bizarre—such a tangled web. Sheryl had blackmailed Langston, because she'd seen him kill Wendell. She confessed that what Ralph did to Debra and Kathy didn't concern her. But after Debra's death, Sheryl only wanted justice. She didn't want any more of Langston's blood money.

She'd lured Laurel down to the swimming hole to tell her about Langston killing Wendell. But she'd panicked when Fred showed up.

Laurel took a deep breath. Finally, it was over. Wendell Vance had gotten justice. But Ralph Langston paid for his crime with his life, and at least three other lives were destroyed by the secrets that had been kept for ten years.

Laurel's suitcase was already in the car. She took one last look around the room at the B&B to be sure she hadn't left anything behind—other than her heart. She blinked against the stinging in her eyes. Nothing she could do about that.

Her cell phone rang. It was her boss, Mitch Decker.

"You got the rest of the evidence?" he asked.

"Yes, sir. Cade has it. It confirms almost everything. It was Debra Honeycutt's hand in the photo. Sheryl Posey will testify that she saw Ralph choke Wendell in return for immunity on extortion charges for the years she blackmailed him. Kathy is pleading to three counts of assault, one of assault with intent and one of manslaughter."

"What about Debra Honeycutt? Why did Langston kill her?"

"We never got to ask him. I guess he found out that she was planning to tell me everything. It's all so tragic. I almost wish I'd never seen that photo."

"You did the right thing," Mitch said. "It sounds like things were coming to a head anyway."

Laurel smiled sadly. "It was like a perfect storm. Kathy and Debra's determination to stop Langston from blackmailing them, Sheryl's efforts to keep the hold she had over him so she could keep his blackmail payments coming in, and his fear that the real truth would come out. So with the reunion as the trigger, and my snooping into the meaning of that picture, it all came together in a tragic climax."

"Right. Don't beat yourself up. You did your job. Now, about Cade Dupree."

Laurel's heart jumped. She'd asked Mitch for a favor, something she'd never done before.

"I had his Quantico file pulled. He was solid. In fact, in several areas he excelled. He got great reviews from his instructors and trainers. A couple of them wrote letters of commendation."

That was Cade. Solid, brilliant, driven to excel. She held her breath.

"It wouldn't be easy—might not even be possible. He was given his first choice of assignment when he graduated. Almost nobody gets their first choice. And he turned it down."

Laurel wanted to blurt out that his brother had died and his father had suffered a stroke, but she bit her tongue. Mitch knew the circumstances.

"He could be assigned anywhere."

Her heart leapt into her throat. Was Mitch saying there was a chance? "I—I don't think he'd mind."

"When would he be ready to move—if he got in?"

She swallowed. "I haven't exactly talked to him. I was just asking."

"I see." Mitch paused, and Laurel felt the criticism in his silence. "Well, if *he* is interested, have him contact me. Meanwhile, are you sure you don't need a couple of days—"

"*No!* I mean, no thank you, sir. I'm ready to get back to work. I've had enough of Dusty Springs, Mississippi." Even as she said it she knew it was a lie. She didn't love the town she'd grown up in, but it was breaking her heart to leave Cade.

"Okay then. See you tomorrow."

"Mitch? Thanks." She hung up.

A quiet cough startled her.

"Had enough of Dusty Springs? I know what you mean."

She turned around. Cade was standing in the open doorway of her room. His face under his tan was pale and his left arm was in a sling. But he was the most beautiful thing she'd ever seen.

Not that it mattered.

"How—what are you doing here?" she finally managed to ask.

He gestured with his head at the open door. "Wide open."

"Oh, right. I was loading the car." She nodded toward his shoulder. "Are you okay?"

"It hurts, but yeah. I'm fine." He pinned her with his blue eyes. "*Who* haven't you exactly talked to?"

Her ears burned with embarrassment. "How long were you standing there listening to me?"

"That was the first thing I heard. So—is it me? Is there something you were going to talk to me about?"

"You think you're the only person I could possibly have been talking about?"

He shrugged, then winced. "Want me to get that bag for you? Your hand—"

"No." Thank goodness he was off the subject of who she hadn't asked what. "Absolutely not. Gunshot trumps a cut on the hand. I'll take it out. I need to get going."

He looked at his watch. "Your plane doesn't leave for four hours."

"There's the drive, and then the check-in…"

"All of which will take about an hour and a half." Cade narrowed his gaze as he assessed Laurel. She was nervous as a long-tailed cat in a room full of rocking chairs. Was she that eager to leave? He knew she harbored no love for Dusty Springs, but he'd like to think she was reluctant to leave him.

Hell. She had a whole life back in D.C. Of course she was ready to go.

What he'd heard her say to her boss still fascinated him though. What business had she left unattended in this town she hated? He knew what he hoped might cause her to want to stay, but he also knew it would never work. He loved her. But that was *his* problem.

She'd never let herself fall for a hometown boy. She'd said it herself. She hated Dusty Springs.

He followed her out to her rental car, taking one last look at her sexy figure, bouncy dark red hair and determined, no-nonsense gait.

He tried to help her load her bags into the trunk, but she ignored him. She opened the driver's side door, but before she could climb in, he took hold of the door. She turned, startled.

"Laurel, is there something you want to say to me?"

Her eyes flickered. "Th-thank you?"

"Come on, Gillespie. Give me a break. Are you just going to drive off without talking about what's between us?"

"Between us?"

"You haven't spoken two words to me since you moved back to the bed-and-breakfast two days ago."

"Cade, I'm so sorry about looking at your letter from the FBI. I never meant to snoop."

His heart sank in disappointment. So that was her unfinished business. *Apologizing.* His defenses rose, trying to shield his heart. "But you did."

"I know and I apologize. Have you—" She stopped, and he saw her throat move as she swallowed. "Have you ever thought about going back?"

"Back?"

"To the FBI."

Her words echoed through him like a pinball machine on tilt. "That's not possible."

She looked down at her feet, then raised her gaze to his. To his surprise her eyes were damp.

The way she was acting scared him. What was she about to say?

"You know I never wanted to come back here. The only reason I let Misty talk me into coming was because of the picture. I had to find out what had really happened to Wendell. But I was determined to get in and out of Dusty Springs without getting any dust on me."

He opened his mouth but she held up her hand.

"If you don't let me finish I'll never get this out." She took a deep breath. "One huge reason I didn't want to ever come back here is because in high school I had the biggest, most desperate crush on an older boy. I knew coming back would hurt. And what I was afraid of is exactly what happened. I was just as smitten as I'd been back then—more so."

"James." He held his breath. He couldn't believe how much it hurt to know that she'd had a crush on James. Or maybe what hurt was that she'd never gotten over his brother.

"James?" Laurel stared at him, her hazel eyes glittering in the noonday sun. "No. It was never James."

He frowned. "But what about the homecoming dance— what the CeeGees did and how much it hurt you? Why did they target you unless they knew you had a crush on him?"

"Because that's what they did. And because to them I was an easy target."

"But if it wasn't James, then who—?" Cade's voice gave out.

Laurel's lips were trembling and tears were gathering in her eyes. "These last few days made me realize I've fallen in love with a solid, honorable, wonderful man who never knew I existed and apparently still doesn't."

He couldn't stop staring at her. He watched a tear slide down her cheek to come to rest at the corner of her mouth. He wanted more than anything to lean forward and kiss it away.

She held up her hand. "So, now that I've humiliated myself, let me get going. I need to get to Memphis."

He caught her hand and pulled her close enough that he could bend his head and capture the tear on his tongue.

She closed her eyes against the poignant pleasure of breathing in his rain-fresh scent.

"Think there's any hope for the solid, honorable lunkhead?" he whispered against her mouth.

"I don't know," she croaked. "Maybe we can ask him."

He gathered her into his arms and kissed her deeply and thoroughly. By the time he'd finished, she was flushed and dewy-eyed.

"I love you, Special Agent Gillespie."

"You do? But it's only been three days."

He shrugged and shook his head. "Once I make up my mind, my dad says I can be pretty stubborn."

"He's right about that. Oh, Chief Dupree. I love you."

He pressed his forehead against hers. "Of course you know we've got a problem."

"I was thinking we had more like a couple dozen problems, but I'll be happy to settle for one. What is it?"

"I don't know about you—but I want to do this right. You know, marriage, the whole bit. But there's one huge obstacle."

She rubbed her forehead lightly against his, but he felt her arms tense.

"What obstacle is that?" she asked quietly.

He leaned back so he could watch her face. He wanted to catch her first unguarded expression when he mentioned the problem. "You're a big-shot FBI agent in Washington, D.C., and I'm a small town police chief in Dusty Springs, Mississippi."

To his surprise, Laurel's face transformed. Her cheeks flamed and she looked happy and nervous and excited all at the same time. "There may be a solution, if you think you could consider relocating," she said. She looked at her watch. "I wonder if I can switch my plane reservation to a later flight."

"I don't suppose you can just cancel it?"

"No. I do have a job to get back to. But before I can leave, you and I have a lot to discuss."

"Like what?"

"Like that letter and my boss. But most of all—like you and me, Dupree." She tossed the car keys onto the front seat of the rental car and threw herself into the strong, safe arms of the man she loved.

* * * * *

Silhouette Desire kicks off 2009 with
MAN OF THE MONTH, *a yearlong program*
featuring incredible heroes by stellar authors.

When navy SEAL Hunter Cabot returns home for
some much-needed R & R, he discovers he's a
married man. There's just one problem: he's never
met his "bride."

Enjoy this sneak peek at Maureen Child's
AN OFFICER AND A MILLIONAIRE.
Available January 2009 from Silhouette Desire.

One

Hunter Cabot, Navy SEAL, had a healing bullet wound in his side, thirty days' leave and, apparently, a wife he'd never met.

On the drive into his hometown of Springville, California, he stopped for gas at Charlie Evans's service station. That's where the trouble started.

"Hunter! Man, it's good to see you! Margie didn't tell us you were coming home."

"Margie?" Hunter leaned back against the front fender of his black pickup truck and winced as his side gave a small twinge of pain. Silently then, he watched as the man he'd known since high school filled his tank.

Charlie grinned, shook his head and pumped gas. "Guess your wife was lookin' for a little 'alone' time with you, huh?"

"My—" Hunter couldn't even say the word. *Wife?* He didn't have a wife. "Look, Charlie..."

"Don't blame her, of course," his friend said with a wink as he finished up and put the gas cap back on. "You being gone all the time with the SEALs must be hard on the ol' love life."

He'd never had any complaints, Hunter thought, frowning at the man still talking a mile a minute. "What're you—"

"Bet Margie's anxious to see you. She told us all about that R & R trip you two took to Bali." Charlie's dark brown eyebrows lifted and wiggled.

"Charlie..."

"Hey, it's okay, you don't have to say a thing, man."

What the hell could he say? Hunter shook his head, paid for his gas and as he left, told himself Charlie was just losing it. Maybe the guy had been smelling gas fumes too long.

But as it turned out, it wasn't just Charlie. Stopped at a red light on Main Street, Hunter glanced out his window to smile at Mrs. Harker, his second-grade teacher who was now at least a hundred years old. In the middle of the crosswalk, the old lady stopped and shouted, "Hunter Cabot, you've got yourself a wonderful wife. I hope you appreciate her."

Scowling now, he only nodded at the old woman—the only teacher who'd ever scared the crap out of him. What the hell was going on here? Was everyone but him nuts?

His temper beginning to boil, he put up with a few more comments about his "wife" on the drive through town before finally pulling into the wide, circular drive leading to the Cabot mansion. Hunter didn't have a clue what was going on, but he planned to get to the bottom of it. Fast.

He grabbed his duffel bag, stalked into the house and paid no attention to the housekeeper, who ran at him, fluttering both hands. "Mr. Hunter!"

"Sorry, Sophie," he called out over his shoulder as he took the stairs two at a time. "Need a shower, then we'll talk."

He marched down the long, carpeted hallway to the rooms that were always kept ready for him. In his suite, Hunter tossed the duffel down and stopped dead. The shower in his bathroom was running. His *wife?*

Anger and curiosity boiled in his gut, creating a

churning mass that had him moving forward without even thinking about it. He opened the bathroom door to a wall of steam and the sound of a woman singing—off-key. Margie, no doubt.

Well, if she was his wife... Hunter walked across the room, yanked the shower door open and stared in at a curvy, naked, temptingly wet woman.

She whirled to face him, slapping her arms across her naked body while she gave a short, terrified scream.

Hunter smiled. "Hi, honey. I'm home."

* * * * *

Be sure to look for
AN OFFICER AND A MILLIONAIRE
by USA TODAY *bestselling author Maureen Child.*
Available January 2009 from Silhouette Desire.

SPECIAL EDITION™

USA TODAY bestselling author
MARIE FERRARELLA

FORTUNES OF TEXAS:
RETURN TO RED ROCK

PLAIN JANE AND THE PLAYBOY

To kill time at a New Year's party, playboy Jorge Mendoza shows the host's teenage son how to woo the ladies. The random target of Jorge's charms: wallflower Jane Gilliam. But with one kiss at midnight, introverted Jane turns the tables on this would-be Casanova, as the commitment-phobe falls for her hook, line and sinker!

*Available January 2009
wherever you buy books.*

REQUEST YOUR FREE BOOKS!

2 FREE NOVELS PLUS 2 FREE GIFTS!

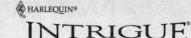

HARLEQUIN®

INTRIGUE®

Breathtaking Romantic Suspense

YES! Please send me 2 FREE Harlequin Intrigue® novels and my 2 FREE gifts (gifts are worth about $10). After receiving them, if I don't wish to receive any more books, I can return the shipping statement marked "cancel." If I don't cancel, I will receive 6 brand-new novels every month and be billed just $4.24 per book in the U.S. or $4.99 per book in Canada, plus 25¢ shipping and handling per book and applicable taxes, if any*. That's a savings of close to 15% off the cover price! I understand that accepting the 2 free books and gifts places me under no obligation to buy anything. I can always return a shipment and cancel at any time. Even if I never buy another book from Harlequin, the two free books and gifts are mine to keep forever.

182 HDN EEZ7   382 HDN EEZK

Name	(PLEASE PRINT)	
Address		Apt. #
City	State/Prov.	Zip/Postal Code

Signature (if under 18, a parent or guardian must sign)

Mail to the **Harlequin Reader Service:**
IN U.S.A.: P.O. Box 1867, Buffalo, NY 14240-1867
IN CANADA: P.O. Box 609, Fort Erie, Ontario L2A 5X3

Not valid to current subscribers of Harlequin Intrigue books.

Want to try two free books from another line?
Call 1-800-873-8635 or visit www.morefreebooks.com.

* Terms and prices subject to change without notice. N.Y. residents add applicable sales tax. Canadian residents will be charged applicable provincial taxes and GST. Offer not valid in Quebec. This offer is limited to one order per household. All orders subject to approval. Credit or debit balances in a customer's account(s) may be offset by any other outstanding balance owed by or to the customer. Please allow 4 to 6 weeks for delivery. Offer available while quantities last.

Your Privacy: Harlequin is committed to protecting your privacy. Our Privacy Policy is available online at www.eHarlequin.com or upon request from the Reader Service. From time to time we make our lists of customers available to reputable third parties who may have a product or service of interest to you. If you would prefer we not share your name and address, please check here. ☐

HI08R

Inside ROMANCE

Stay up-to-date on all your romance reading news!

The Inside Romance newsletter is a FREE quarterly newsletter highlighting our upcoming series releases and promotions!

Click on the <u>Inside Romance</u> link on the front page of **www.eHarlequin.com** or e-mail us at insideromance@harlequin.ca to sign up to receive your FREE newsletter today!

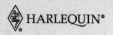

INTRIGUE

COMING NEXT MONTH

#1107 FAMILIAR VOWS by Caroline Burnes
Fear Familiar
Familiar's back! The crime-solving black cat detective was on the case of a killer targeting beautiful wedding photographer Michelle Sieck. But neither the killer nor Michelle knew they'd each have to go toe to toe with U.S. Marshal Lucas West.

#1108 SECRETS IN FOUR CORNERS by Debra Webb
Kenner County Crime Unit
Sheriff Patrick Martinez was the law in these parts of Colorado, and nobody was going to be intimidated under his watch—least of all his longtime love Bree Hunter and her little daughter, who he wished was his....

#1109 THE NIGHT IN QUESTION by Kelsey Roberts
The Rose Tattoo
For the life of her, Kresley Hayes could not explain how her unconscious body washed up on the shore in an evening gown. Lucky for her, FBI Agent Matthew DeMarco found her. Inexplicably reluctant to turn to the law for help, Kresley had to decide whether she could trust the handsome Matt with her life, let alone her heart.

#1110 BRANDED BY THE SHERIFF by Delores Fossen
Texas Paternity: Boots and Babies
When a family feud led to brutal murders in this Texas town, it was up to Sheriff Beck Tanner to protect single mother Faith Matthews and her baby from the killer. But Beck didn't expect to feel such fierce protectiveness over mother and child, especially when saving their lives meant facing off with his own family...

#1111 A VOICE IN THE DARK by Jenna Ryan
He's a Mystery
A serial killer's brutal attack left criminal profiler Noah Graydon scarred and determined to stay concealed from the world—that was, until he met Angel Carter, beautiful FBI agent and the killer's next target.

#1112 BETTER THAN BULLETPROOF by Kay Thomas
Ex-marine Harlan Jeffries thought he could handle anything...but when he found himself in the unlikely position of dodging bullets for Gina Rodgers and her orphaned nephew, he knew that more than his extreme protective instincts were motivating his actions.

HICNM1208BPA